Indebted Epilogue

INDEBTED #7

PEPPER WINTERS

Published: Pepper Winters 2015: **pepperwinters@gmail.com**
Cover Design: by Ari at Cover it! Designs:
http://salon.io/#coveritdesigns
Proofreading by: Jenny Sims: **http://www.editing4indies.com**
Images in Manuscript from Canstock Photos:
http://www.canstockphoto.com

OTHER WORK BY PEPPER WINTERS

Pepper Winters is a New York Times, Wall Street Journal, and USA Today International Bestseller.

Her Dark Romance books include:
Monsters in the Dark Trilogy
Tears of Tess (Monsters in the Dark #1)
Quintessentially Q (Monsters in the Dark #2)
Twisted Together (Monsters in the Dark #3)

Indebted Series
Debt Inheritance (Indebted #1)
First Debt (Indebted Series #2)
Second Debt (Indebted Series #3)
Third Debt (Indebted Series #4)
Fourth Debt (Indebted Series #5)
Final Debt (Indebted Series #6)
Indebted Epilogue (Indebted Series #7)

Her Grey Romance books include:
Destroyed
Ruin & Rule (Pure Corruption MC #1)
Sin & Suffer (Pure Corruption MC #2)

Her Upcoming Releases include:
2016: **Je Suis a Toi (Monsters in the Dark Novella)**
January 2016: **Sin & Suffer (Pure Corruption MC #2)**
2016: **Super Secret Series**
2016: **Unseen Messages (Standalone Romance)**
2016: **Indebted Beginnings (Indebted Series Prequel)**

To be the first to know of upcoming releases, please follow her on her website
Pepper Winters

KITE007: *COME TO bed.*

Needle&Thread: *I'm working. Almost finished on this dress.*

Kite007: *I don't care. Come to bed. My cock is hard. My arms are empty. I want to fuck you.*

Needle&Thread: *So bossy.*

Kite007: *And you're back to being a tease with your naughty nun outfit.*

Needle&Thread: *I'm neither a tease nor a nun. For your information, I've been designing a very important outfit tonight.*

Kite007: *Teasing again. I might have to come down there and spank you.*

Needle&Thread: *You can spank me, but not here. You're not allowed to see.*

Kite007: *Now I'm hard and pissed off. What are you hiding from me?*

Needle&Thread: *My wedding dress, oh so impatient husband-to-be. Or did you forget about our marriage next week?*

Kite007: *Fuck. Say that again.*

Needle&Thread: *What? Marriage? Wedding Dress? Husband-to-be? I'm going to be your wife soon; you have to stop being so demanding by text message. Otherwise, I'll just delete your number.*

Kite007: *Your teasing is driving me insane. I'm touching myself,*

Needle. I want you lips where my hand is and my tongue between your legs.

Needle&Thread: *I want that, too.*

Kite007: *Come to bed.*

Needle&Thread: *I have a better idea. Come find me. Come claim me. Come fuck me as your naughty nun before I become your wife.*

Kite007: *Your wish is my command…better start running, little Weaver. I won't be gentle when I find you.*

Jethro

Three Months Before...

HAWKSRIDGE HALL REMAINED the same but slowly evolved as more minutes passed. Furniture that'd seen countless generations bound by contracts were no longer clouded with debts and ill wishes. Drapes and tapestries that'd witnessed countless days of sadness, suddenly looked upon freedom. Weavers lived with Hawks and no debts or screams collected.

Rooms were transformed, Bonnie's parlour renovated, and the drab and dreary aura dispelled.

Bonnie had done a lot of wrong, but training Jasmine was not one of them. My sister's lessons were exemplary and together we took on the mammoth task of running the estate.

I was heir but I willingly shared the role. Primogeniture and old-fashioned standings had no bearing on us anymore.

Together, we patched up the Hall and put bygones with bygones. However, there was one thing I had to do myself. The hastily-written Will and video declaration from Cut superseded the previous ruling of his death ever being suspicious. I travelled on my own to a new lawyer firm. Not the ones who'd looked after my family's interests and debt catalogue for generations. I had plans for that firm. I would deal with them soon enough.

In the meantime, I wanted new contacts—above board and legal.

After shadowy background and vague description of my father's wishes, I lodged the updated version with them with their assurances they would ensure Hawksridge and my future wouldn't be harmed.

One more thing off my list, but so many still to go.

I also strengthened our alliance with the local authorities to ensure no more nasty misunderstandings and assured them Vaughn's prank with social media and public nuisance wouldn't happen again.

Returning to the Hall, I sought out Nila for comfort.

Whenever we were apart, dealing with life and difficulties, I missed her. Without even realising it, she'd become my world, my salvation, and my heart never stopped skipping whenever she was close.

My quarters were empty without her. My arms were useless without her in them.

The past couple of months, I'd grown used to having her in my bed, showering in my bathroom, and leaving her half-finished creations in little heaps around the room.

She had quirks I found endearing. Habits I adored.

I fucking loved her.

Everything about her.

My condition hadn't grown easier to bear. Leaving the estate and dealing with strangers was the hardest part. Listening to emotions I had no right to listen to. Feeling arguments and worry from people I didn't know stripped me bare, ensuring I drained Nila when I had her back in my arms.

I couldn't watch TV or relax with a movie. I barely tolerated music.

But Nila tolerated me.

For some reason, she didn't mind when I told her to be quiet and just let me hold her. She didn't argue when I took her silently to bed and teased her mercilessly so I could settle into the lust and desire she felt for me.

She gave me everything with nothing barred.

She made me more whole and centred than I'd ever been.

She made me...better.

THREE MONTHS HAD passed since everything ended.

Three months since Kestrel died.

Three months since Jethro stopped his birthright and the Debt Inheritance.

Jethro dealt with lawyers and other estate business. Jasmine ran the household. My father helped clear away evidence of the ballroom bloodbath and paid the mercenaries who had helped save my life.

We were all busy, traipsing onward, living…

Hawksridge was no longer a mausoleum housing smugglers and psychopaths—its halls were now light and airy, its rooms full of tentative laughter and love.

Spinning my black diamond engagement ring, I smiled. We hadn't set a date yet but life had been good to us. Tex had renewed his efforts to find Jacqueline, and Vaughn had been a regular visitor to see Jasmine. We'd all found a place within this new world.

A gentle tap on the greenhouse octagon door wrenched my head up.

Jethro had left me for an hour to deal with more paperwork. The requirement of running such a large estate was never ending.

I would be lying if I said entering the muggy warmth had

been easy. The scars on my back twinged. The crack of the whip as Jethro hit me for the First Debt hovering in the stagnant air.

Orchids and white jasmine perfumed the air, granting peace where before there'd been only pain. I hadn't been back since that day, but it didn't give me nightmares with unresolved issues.

I found closure by trailing my fingers on the post where Jethro had tied me. I smiled softly as I weaved old memories with new—knowing my plan of making him care had worked.

We'd begun this as enemies, fighting against each other.

But we'd ended up as partners, stopping the war side by side.

The tapping noise came again, hidden by foliage on the other side of the octagon.

I stood up just as Jethro stepped into the room, his golden eyes more amber honey in the gentle sunshine of the glasshouse.

"I looked for you in our wing." Jethro's gaze narrowed on the whipping post in the centre of the octagon. Newly budded flowers and juvenile vines helped hide its original occupation. "I never expected to find you in here."

Moving toward me, his touch landed on my shoulders, digging deep with need and love. "You okay?"

Sunlight highlighted his silvering hair, glittering like some expensive thread. His cheekbones cut shadows, his brow etched with contours. And his lips...his lips were slightly parted and damp from his tongue.

Ever since Cut had taken his last breath, Jethro had changed. Not significantly but enough to notice subtle evolutions. He held himself higher, not proud like the rightful heir to his fortune, but like a man no longer crippled with negativity and hatred seeping from the air.

He looked younger, wiser, calmer, gentler.

I smiled softly, lifting my hand in invitation. "I am now you're here."

His fingers slinked through mine, sending arcs of electricity into my heart. He squeezed, bending his elegant legs to sit beside me, dragging me back to the bench.

I sat willingly, melting into his side, inhaling his unique scent of woods and leather.

Hip to hip, thigh to thigh, our hearts beat to the same rhythm.

Sighing contentedly, I snuggled into him, kissing his throat as his arm wrapped around my shoulders, gluing me tighter against him. "What are you thinking about?"

I closed my eyes, letting the gentle warmth of late spring's sunshine eradicate any leftover history. "You can't tell?"

Jethro shook his head. "It's scrambled. You're sad but not. Happy but calm." He pulled away, looking into my eyes. "You're focusing on too much too fast."

My lips twitched. "Ah, finally a way to fool you. I was beginning to think I'd never be able to keep a secret."

His face darkened. "You promised there would be no need for secrets." Anxiety stiffened his body. "Is everything...okay?" He waved at the room. "Did you come here for a reason? Do you still hate me for that day? For hurting you so much?" His voice lowered with regret. "Fuck, Nila. I'd give anything to rewind the clock and—"

"Shush." I cupped my hand over his mouth. His five o'clock shadow rasped beneath my palm. "Everything is fine. I'm just...sitting still. If that makes sense. I'm letting my thoughts wander without thinking, finding ends to things that need to be finished."

Imprisoning my wrist with his fingers, he tugged my hand away from his mouth. "That makes perfect sense."

His fingers drew lazy circles on my inner wrist, sending delicious shivers over my skin. Looking at the blooming flowers and exotic breeds, he fell silent.

For a while, we didn't say anything, both of us lost in our own thoughts. Every breath I took scattered rainbow-diamonds over our laps. My Weaver Wailer—or should I say Hawk

Redeemer—was the last piece, the final symbol that the past few months weren't a nightmare but real.

And I'd survived them.

Even if there was a way to get it off, I didn't want to. I'd grown accustomed to the weight. I wore its fracturing rainbows with pride, and I liked the thought of the diamonds being my friend instead of my enemy, gracing my body until I took my last inhale.

Jethro kissed the top of my head. "I have something for you."

"Oh?" I pulled away, looking into his gorgeous face. "Do I need to be worried?" My thoughts filled with teasing. We'd all been so serious; it was time to play again. My lips spread as I asked, "Is it time for another de—"

"If you ask me if it's another debt, I'll put you over my knee right here and spank you." His voice flirted with gruff and sexy.

My eyes flittered to the post, a coy smirk widening. "You know you could spank me on the pole and replace the First Debt with a better ending."

His throat contracted as he swallowed. "What better ending?" His eyes flashed dark. "If I remember rightly, I almost raped you after that debt. I felt sick to my fucking stomach for ever thinking that way, let alone being turned on by hurting you."

He looked away, shaking his head in disgust. "I don't understand how I got off on that. How I could ignore your pain and find anything remotely erotic about it." He curled his lips. "You called me a sadist, remember? I refuted it, but once I'd finished tending to your back, I wondered if you were right. How could someone like me—someone who's gone his entire life absorbing other's thoughts—suddenly be turned on by another's agony?"

My heart fluttered. I hadn't given it much thought. But the more I studied Jethro's abhorrent self-confession, the more an answer unfurled inside my mind.

He felt what others did. He had no choice. And yet he'd still been under the influence of Cut's conditioning just enough to block out avalanches of sensation.

Would it make sense he'd picked up select thoughts? Drank in my desire for him, my aching, burning need when he'd taunted me with history and barely-given kisses?

I looked at my fingers, twining together in my lap. "I think I know why."

His eyes shot to me, his eyebrows raised with questions. "Know what?"

"Why you were turned on that day."

He tensed. "It was a sick thing to do. Out of everything I did to you, masturbating on your back still fills me with shame. I wish I could take it back."

Twisting to face him, I stroked his cheek. "Before you berate yourself, stop and think. Did you never question why you desperately needed to come? Why you wanted me so badly?"

He froze.

I laughed. "Come on, Kite. You know your condition inside and out, and you're telling me you can't figure what caused that minor incident?"

He growled, "It was hardly minor."

Not waiting for me to reply, he soared upright, untangling himself to pace. "I don't understand. What are you saying?"

I stood too, smiling as if I had the secret to everything— which, in a way, I had. I thought he'd figured it out that day. That was why he'd been kind to me afterward, why he'd softened even when he was told not to. "You enjoyed hurting me that day because of me."

"Yes, because of you," he snarled. "I got so fucking hard over you. And I hated you for it. You made me enjoy your pain when I normally run from feeling anything remotely intense."

"Exactly."

Jethro slammed to a stop. "You're not making any sense. Spit it out."

I moved toward him. "You felt what I felt. Yes, it hurt. Yes, that whip was my worst nightmare and the lashes felt like a bazillion bees stinging my back, but before it grew too painful, I wanted you. God, I wanted you. I was so wet. If you'd stopped after a couple of strikes, I wouldn't have fought you. I would've willingly spread my legs and taken you because all I could think about was how much I needed you."

Jethro's mouth fell open. "You're saying I fed off what you were feeling that entire time?"

"Toward the end, I'll admit I hated you. I wanted more than anything for it to stop, and when you tried to take me, it was the last thing I wanted to happen. But, Jethro, before that. I genuinely craved for you to touch me. I begged for it. But you never cracked. You wouldn't even kiss me."

"Fuck." He dragged a hand over his face. "I honestly thought I'd lost it. For months, I feared who I'd become because of what happened that day. I stayed away from you for weeks afterward, because I didn't trust myself. I thought I'd get off on hurting you more. I was fucking terrified I'd finally turned into Cut."

My heart beat harder for him, wishing I'd known so I could've comforted him. Then again, we weren't exactly friends yet. He'd suffered on his own, but perhaps that was the way it had to be for him to finally realise there was something rich and deep and undeniable between us.

"I guess there's a lot of things we need to go back over and put to rest."

His arms lassoed around me tightly. "I think you're right." Nuzzling my hair, he murmured, "How about we go to each place where the debts were completed and replace them with a happier memory."

I hugged him back. "I'd like that."

Sex to replace the First Debt.

A lakeside picnic to replace the Second Debt.

My mind skipped to the Third Debt—the debt that would've broken me if it weren't for Kestrel protecting me by being such a gentleman. At the time, I'd been conflicted, hurt Jethro wasn't there, confused as to my body's reaction to Kes.

But now, I was glad we'd had that moment together. I loved Kes. I couldn't admit it before as I didn't fully understand it, but I loved him more than a friend but less than Jethro. A friend who would always have my heart.

Jethro sighed, knowing where my thoughts were without me having to vocalize.

His condition truly took any secrecy out of our relationship. I would never be able to hide anything, and in some ways, it annoyed me. I would never be able to sulk behind white lies or indulge in a cold shoulder if we ever had a fight.

But at the same time, it was refreshing to know there would never be anything between us because his gift worked both ways. Yes, he could feel what I felt, but at the same time, I could read him better than he knew. His eyes, his face, his body—they all told me what I needed to know.

Jethro cupped the back of my nape, running his fingers along my throat and collar. "I know what Kes did to you that night. At the time, I fucking hated him for it, but now...I'm actually glad you had that with him. You deserved to know how much he cared for you."

I nodded. "Me too. It was wrong in a way but right as well. It doesn't mean I love you any less, but there'll always be space for Kes in my heart."

Jethro smiled sadly. "As it should. He was part of me, my only true confidant. I'm glad you'll miss him as much as me." His head tilted, lips coming to meet mine.

We stood still as we kissed softly.

His tongue licked my bottom lip, and I opened for him. Inhaling his soul and taste, I slipped into bone-sated happiness knowing I belonged to this man and he belonged to me.

I was no longer alone.

I would never be alone again.

We'd bound ourselves together and become family.

VAUGHN

I WON'T SAY it was easy. Because it wasn't.

I won't say everything became fucking puppies and rainbows. Because it didn't.

The pain was still there.

The knowledge my father was broken, my mother murdered, and an unknown sister given away at birth.

But things did get easier.

Tex slowly grew used to Threads and Jethro together. He'd watch them touch and whisper and even he couldn't deny their love was pure.

Jethro had been a cocksucker; he'd hurt my sister and almost destroyed my family, but he'd done everything in his power to fix his wrongs and ensure he earned the right to forgiveness. It helped that he loved Threads so fucking much. He lit up around her. He became *more* around her. He breathed because of her.

In a way, I was fucking jealous. He'd stolen her from me completely. They shone around each other, and when I caught him watching her, the aching adoration in his gaze made me admit Nila was lucky.

She would never be alone or unloved again. She'd met the one who would be there for her through night and day, happy and sad, bad and good.

He would be there for her even when death came for them.

I, on the other hand, grew restless living on someone else's turf. I loved patching my family back together and enjoyed the night chats I had with Jasmine. But I missed the magic of London, the thrill of running the company—the real world.

I returned to my apartment in the city a couple of weeks after Kestrel's funeral. Tex moved back to the family home, returning to the factory as if nothing life-changing had happened. Jethro had given me an open invitation to come and stay at the Hall as often as I liked. And Nila said she'd miss me but her place was now with her Hawk.

I was fine with all of it.

However, it was Jasmine who shocked everyone.

She admitted she wanted to leave Hawksridge and explore a new life.

Jethro had almost fucking passed out hearing his baby sister, a self-confessed recluse, wanted to leave the estate.

She wouldn't tell me the story of how she lost the use of her legs, but I knew it had something to do with her brother and father. I wanted to know her secrets, but then again, so much was in the past that it was best to let it go and move forward.

The argument about Jasmine's living arrangements had lasted a full night before Jethro conceded he couldn't keep his sister prisoner—no matter how much he would fret over her safety.

I'd almost spat out my tea when Jaz calmly turned to me and asked if she could move in with me for a time.

Fuck.

I'd gone from a bachelor flirting with the sister of the man about to become my brother-in-law to inheriting a live-in girlfriend.

I'd be lying if I said I didn't put the moves on Jasmine. I'd kissed her. I wanted her. But she wouldn't let me go any further. I knew she was a virgin, and she was worried about her body and disability. But I didn't care about that. Fuck, all I cared about was hearing her laugh and making her come with my tongue.

As for her request, I didn't have to think about it. Of course, I agreed. And the next day, we moved out of Hawksridge. I stole a Hawk to share my home.

Luckily, I had a penthouse in downtown London. Lifts serviced the floors and the extra-wide corridors proved to be the perfect environment for her to get around.

We became friends.

Great friends.

More than friends.

I wanted her every evening we spent ribbing each other watching crap TV. I needed her every day we argued over which model would be best to showcase Nila's show pieces. My cock hardened constantly around her, yet she never insinuated sex and I didn't want to scare her by pushing.

For months, we lived together and never crossed the line.

I honestly didn't know if she could even have sex. Would she be able to feel me? Would she even want me to see her naked, to bring her pleasure and fulfil the prophecy she herself had decreed the night she'd rolled into my life and demanded my help to save her dying brothers.

She'd said one day I would belong to a woman other than my sister.

At the time, I'd wanted to rip out her fucking heart for ever suggesting such a thing. I was a Weaver. Loyal and true. But what she'd said was right. Life moved on, we grew up, and eventually, we all replaced our blood families with chosen ones.

And somehow, Jasmine became my chosen one.

She enticed me more and more.

I wanted her more and fucking more.

If only she would give in to me. If only she trusted me that I wanted her because of her mind and soul and not just her body.

She wouldn't submit…not yet.

But I wouldn't stop trying.

And the day she finally gave in…she would make me the

happiest fucking man in the world.

Three Months and One Week Later...

LIFE WAS FULL of moments and this was the biggest of all.

Today was the end of my godforsaken life and the first day of a pristine existence.

For three months, I'd found the happiness I never dared dream of. Hawksridge Hall came alive with companionship and friendship rather than lust and greed. Flaw managed the Black Diamond brothers with ease. Our smuggling was no more; we'd opened the lines for proper trade with diamonds, ensuring our mines and workers were well compensated.

Nila and I had returned to *Almasi Kipanga*. We'd given every worker bonuses, set up fair work practices, and arranged a proper building estate to be erected to house those who wanted to stay.

Once completed, we sent word to our other mines: emeralds in Thailand, rubies in Burma. The other Black Diamond factions changed their practices to better suit our loyal workers.

The new regime was named after the man who'd planned all along to improve our employees' conditions: Kestrel.

While in Botswana, we also overturned Cut's commands

that any worker injured in the mine had to leave. We tracked down those employees and rehired all those he'd fired and rehabilitated those who'd lost limbs in tragic accidents. We also compensated the families who'd lost loved ones working for us. Money couldn't bring back their family, but it could make their future a little easier.

Vaughn and Jasmine officially announced they were together, and Tex had finally started to shed some of his guilt.

Together, the Weavers worked to find Jacqueline. Only last week we were told there might be a lead on a woman matching Nila and Vaughn's birthday living not far away in Cornwall.

Things were healing. And Nila had healed me in return.

And now...she'd given me the best gift she could ever do. Married me.

My hands fisted as she appeared at the top of the aisle. All around us, the ocean glistened as the sun set on the most spectacular day.

This had been V's idea. He'd seen the photos I'd doctored when I first stole Nila. The ones of me hugging her on a private yacht and kissing her at sea. He'd jokingly said a couple of months ago when we set the date that our nuptials would have to be on a boat to honour the almost futuristic prediction of those photographs.

I couldn't agree more.

My heart thundered as Nila drifted forward. Her father clutched her tight while his face glowed with pride and love. Her dress was the one she'd refused to let me see the night she didn't come to bed.

She'd somehow conjured exactly what I envisioned. After making love to her that night, the strangest thought popped into my head and never left.

The black gown I'd torn from her when I threw her on my motorcycle had always haunted me. I'd felt what that dress meant to her. The countless hours of hardship and skill she'd poured into the fabric creation. I hadn't let her see how much her despair affected me that night but I wanted to somehow change that memory—just as we'd changed all the others.

Either she'd sensed my desires or I'd picked up on her thoughts of what she busily created—either way, she drifted toward me in the mirror image of the dress, but instead of black, she glistened in silver and white.

My eyes smarted, drinking her in. This was the first time I'd seen the gown but not the first time I'd been teased with it.

Once she finished the dress, she'd called George and Sylvie who'd done the *Vanity Fair* article when Nila had returned to Hawksridge. As promised, they were offered an exclusive release, hiding the gown from me but preparing the four-page spread for the world.

I glanced over at the two reporters, snapping pictures and taking notes on our wedding. Part of the arrangement included coverage of the ceremony so the last nasty rumours were put to rest—along with every other transgression and hardship of the past year.

Vaughn apologised for causing the social media backlash, but I didn't accept his apology. He'd done what he could to save Nila. He was a pain in my arse most days, but he loved his sister, and in turn, I loved him because of that.

George waved his pen in my direction, smiling in his tuxedo.

They were the only invited non-family guests at this wedding.

We'd kept it small—partly because of my condition, but mostly because a marriage was private. Really, it was between two people and that was it. A spectacle didn't need to be made when all we needed was a celebrant, a ring, and a shared vow.

My back straightened as Nila ghosted closer. She looked like a princess, a queen—*my* queen.

White and soft grey feathers covered her cleavage, sewn with immense skill to transform from feather to gemstone further down the bodice.

The hooped skirt swept like a bell as Tex brought his

daughter closer to me, gifting her to me in an age-old tradition.

The first time I'd stolen Nila, I'd threatened him and taken her without his approval. This time, he willingly gave her to me to safeguard because he knew without a doubt I would die for her, I would fight for her…I would change history for her.

The sea breeze caught the edge of her veil, fluttering the lace around her face, activating the large diamond secured in her hair to drench her in rainbows.

The diamond collar gleamed like fire, picking up the orange of the sunset and the flash of white heels peeked under the layers of skirts with every step. The only thing on her that wasn't white was her engagement ring and bracelet.

The black diamonds sucked in what the white diamonds glittered off. The onyx gem absorbed the emotions and celebration of such a day, storing deep within its priceless heart, kept safe forever.

"You're a lucky son of a bitch." V's whispered words came from beside me.

Glancing at him, I grinned. Today was bittersweet. I never thought I would get married. And if I ever found the one to take me on, I envisioned my brother as my best man. Kestrel wasn't there in body, but he was in spirit. I felt his pride on the sea air. I saw his smile in the sunset. And my new brother stood in his place. My brother-in-law.

"I know. Believe me, I know."

Jasmine sat opposite, in the maid of honour position. Her eyes reflected the colour of her beautiful bridesmaid's dress of purple and black. Nila had designed the gown, as well as my suit and V's best man's outfit. We all matched. A family.

The soft music stopped playing as Nila ended the procession within touching distance.

Tex wiped away a tear as he hugged his daughter. He'd lost the weight he'd carried ever since I'd taken Nila and looked like the distinguished gentleman from the night I stole her.

We'd had a private chat a couple of months ago. I'd apologised to him for what my family had done and sworn on the graves of my ancestors that Nila was forever safe in my arms.

Nila stood before me.

I blinked, drinking in her incredible perfection.

Her tiny hands slotted into mine, and I squeezed her so damn hard.

The celebrant I'd hired clasped his fingers together, looking at the small congregation. There weren't many of us. Flaw represented the Black Diamonds. Tex represented Nila's family. There were no business partners or friends, no assistants or organisers.

Just the people who mattered.

"Do you have your own vows or would you like to repeat after me?"

Nila smiled softly. "We've already said what we needed to."

I nodded, thinking about the newly framed Sacramental Pledge hanging in my office. The figurines from my boyhood and the contract for my happiness as an adult, side by side.

"Go ahead with traditional. The sooner she's my wife, the better."

The celebrant smiled, his dark hair catching the sunset as it kissed the ocean. England was behind us. The Greek isles and Santorini nestled us, floating on the turquoise ocean.

Our honeymoon would be spent here. Relaxing on the beach and making love in the moonlight. V and Tex had planned to source some local cotton and silk, while Flaw had meetings with jewellery shops to stock our diamonds.

Work and pleasure.

A perfect combination.

"Do you, Jethro 'Kite' Hawk, take this woman as your lawfully wedded wife, for now and forever, in sickness and in health, for as long as you both shall live?"

I didn't need to think. "I do." *A thousand times, I do.*

"And do you, Nila Threads Weaver, take this man as your lawfully wedded husband, for now and forever, in sickness and in health, for as long as you both shall live?"

Nila shook her head.

Shook her head? *What the fuck?*

Smiling, she murmured, "I take him now and forever but not for as long as we both shall live." She squeezed my fingers, her eyes glinting. "Far beyond that. For eternity."

I couldn't wait for the 'you may kiss the bride' part. I grabbed her shoulders and yanked her forward. My lips met hers, and I forgot about the world and witnesses. I forgot about everything but soldering my soul to this woman who'd captured me as carefully as a net captures a hawk.

Speaking into her mouth, I whispered, "Seeing as you changed the rules, I have another one to add to your vow. I swear to love you forever. You are no longer indebted to me. I'm indebted to you. My heart is in your debt. My happiness. My very life is yours."

Nila melted, holding onto me as I dipped her and deepened the kiss.

Laughing, the celebrant spoke to the gathered crowd. "Seeing as you just sealed your vows, I now pronounce you husband and wife."

The cheers crested, and for the first time in my life, being in a crowd didn't hurt. The overwhelming sensation of everyone's emotions was of happiness, fulfilment, and joy.

Tex enveloped us in a hug. "Welcome to the family, Hawk."

I grinned. "Thank you for having me."

Tex kissed his daughter. "I guess you're no longer a Weaver, Threads."

Nila sighed. "I'll always be your daughter, Dad, but for now, I belong and have willingly become a Hawk."

He nodded as if it made perfect sense that his daughter married the son of the man who killed his wife. It was a twisted world, but somehow, Nila and I had found a way to untangle it to the point of acceptance.

My fingertips tingled from our tally tattoos and I made a

note to ask Nila if she'd like to finish the marks now we'd cemented our lives together. Ten fingers, ten tattoos. A lifetime of happiness.

Somehow, we'd found life over death.

Chosen freedom over debts.

And I would never take my future or my wife for granted.

JETHRO LOCKED THE door.

The yacht rocked beneath our toes, sedate and savage in its sea-cradle.

The curtains had been drawn across the balcony, the bed turned down by well-trained staff, and all the guests remaining on board were a floor below.

We were the only bedroom on this level.

Private.

Alone.

Swiping a hand through his slicked back hair, Jethro traversed the distance between us. We didn't speak as the air intensified and love poured from his heart to mine.

The white gold wedding band I'd had fashioned along with a few black diamonds I'd sourced at Diamond Alley graced his finger—absorbing the light rather than sparkling—sucking its life inward, protecting its secrets.

The matching ring hummed on my finger. The large midnight stone grew heavier the closer Jethro came.

"We did it." His voice teased with disbelief. "We're married."

I nodded, a little breathless and a lot nervous. "We are."

"You're mine."

"I'm yours."

"There are no more debts. No more threats."

I moved toward him, stepping onto the silver rug he stood on. Our bodies swayed as a current rocked the yacht, but our eyes never unlocked. "We're free."

Breathing hard, Jethro reached for me. His arms wrapped around me, gathering me toward him so the white silk of my gown rippled over my skin and floor.

Stars and moon above were the only elements invited into our room. The skylight above had a ladder granting access to the private deck. The nose of the boat was out of bounds to anyone. We could make love down here with the sky as company or make our way upside and fuck with the air licking our skin.

We could travel the world.

We could kiss and touch and never have to hide our happiness from anyone.

We have so much to look forward to.

Jethro's gaze drifted to my collar. His tongue swept over his bottom lip as the faint sparkle of diamonds kissed his chin. "You should know something."

I froze in his arms, my heart rate spiking. "Know what?"

He shifted me in his embrace, cupping my throat with gentle fingers. His thumb ran along the diamonds. "You admitted you didn't want me to find a way to remove this. You'll never wear another necklace as long as you live. No matter where you go. No matter what you do, this collar will be with you every step."

"I know. I want it to be that way." Resting my hands on his hips, I frowned a little, trying to understand his point. "You put it on me, Jethro. It will stay on until I die."

His back tightened, the muscles either side of his spine bunching beneath my fingertips. "That's how I view what happened today."

"What do you mean?"

His forehead furrowed, shadowing his golden eyes. "I mean—marriage to me isn't a simple ceremony and celebration.

Marriage is like your collar. A one-time deal. Never to break, binding us together until death do us part. Just like there will never be another necklace, there will never be goodbye between us. No opportunity to sever what we've found."

My tummy twisted as flutters entered my core. "That's how I view it, too. It wasn't a meaningless vow, Kite. I willingly said the words."

"But do you fully comprehend that this is it? No other men. No flirtations or dalliances. *Me*. I'm the last you'll ever have." His head dropped. "Is that enough for you?"

I laughed softly. I couldn't help it. "You're seriously asking me if you're enough for me?" My heart overflowed. "Jethro you're *too* much. You're everything I could ever hope for. Why are you feeling insecure?" I snuggled closer, pressing my cheek on his lapel, avoiding the diamond pin through the fabric. "After everything we've been through, everything we said today and yesterday, you're afraid I'll divorce you and run?"

Jethro didn't respond. His chest rose and fell, his arms binding tighter as if he didn't trust me not to vanish.

I let silence and the creaking of the yacht ease some of his fear before murmuring, "I suggest you remember the day I ran from you after the welcome luncheon because that's the one and only time I'll ever run away. I chose you with my eyes open, Kite. I know what our connection will mean for you and the struggle I'll sometimes have to keep giving you what you need. But I'm not a little girl. I'm a woman who's chosen her soul-mate. I'm strong enough to love you unconditionally. I'm smart enough to know some days will be good and some days will be bad. And I'm brave enough to solemnly swear that we will be together until the end.

"I don't want anyone else. You're my best friend, my rescuer. You're the man I was born for as decreed by six-hundred-years of pacts. Don't doubt what we have on the eve of what could be the happiest time of our lives."

Jethro suddenly groaned, wrapping his arms so tight he bruised me. "Fuck, I'm sorry. I don't know why I doubted."

"I know why."

He raised my chin with a fingertip. "Why?"

I smiled, loving the way the moonlight highlighted the silver in his hair, making him look part god, part majestic sculpture. "Because everything is so good now. It's hard not to suspect it will all vanish after a lifetime of having everything you loved stripped away."

He paused, biting his inner cheek. "You're right."

"Of course, I'm right."

His lips tilted crookedly. "To this day, I don't know what I did to deserve you, but I'm never letting you go."

"Good." Standing on my tiptoes, I whispered, "Now, enough talk of divorce. Let's enjoy being married first. Stop speaking and take me to bed, Mr. Hawk."

He jolted, a growl escaping. Letting me go, he grabbed my wrist, yanking me toward the towering mattress and turned down sheets. "It would be my pleasure, Ms. Wea—" His mouth shot closed, his eyes clouding.

I knew his thoughts. Mine had already been over the technicalities. My father had changed his last name to match my mother's as per the rules of the Debt Inheritance. By right, Jethro should become a Weaver.

However, I had no intention of stripping the heir of Hawksridge his name. The very name he'd always strived to earn and change for the better.

Sitting on the bed in a shower of white lace, I patted the mattress beside me. "I think the term of address you're looking for is *Mrs.* Hawk."

His eyes shot bronze. "Are you sure? You don't have to take my name. You can keep Weaver if you want—"

"What I want is to belong to you. I want the world to know it. I want the ghosts who battled together for so long to hear it. I want us to become one." Taking his hand, I yanked him beside me. "Try again, only this time, use the right name."

Pressing my shoulders, he slowly guided me onto my back. His breath skated over my mouth as he lowered himself beside me. "I'm going to love you until my heart stops beating and then beyond…Mrs. Hawk."

I shivered. "I'm glad. Because I had the exact same plan, Mr. Hawk."

He grinned, bowing his head to kiss me.

My heart raced as his tongue slipped past my lips, seducing me with slow licks. His fingers slinked into my hair, pulling free pins and clips, letting the black strands cascade into a mess on the sheets. Once every decoration and slide was free, he massaged my scalp, dislodging a few remaining petals from the rice and flower confetti.

"As much as I love you in this dress, I think it's time it disappeared, don't you?"

I nodded.

Jethro was mine in every possible way. He would continue to need me. I would continue to need him. We were no longer on our own but a partnership, lovers…a family.

The stress of the wedding left my bloodstream, relaxing my shoulders into the springy bed.

His hands slipped behind me, rolling me onto my stomach as he set to the task of undoing fifty-two pearl buttons down my back.

The panels of lace decorated my skin, revealing the muscles of my spine and risqué glimpses beneath. I didn't think I'd have time to sew something so delicate, but it'd been cathartic for me to sketch and create something so stunningly simple but intricately beautiful.

Goosebumps erupted as Jethro's knuckles brushed my skin, slowly releasing me from the gown. Half-way down my back, he swallowed a groan. "Goddammit, I want to rip this off you. This is taking far too long."

I laughed into the sheets. "You rip it and I'll make you fix it. Patience is a virtue, husband."

His touch halted. "What did you call me?"

I looked over my shoulder. "Husband." Loving the way his eyes hooded, I breathed, "That's what you are now.

Husband. *My* husband."

His mouth parted, dangerous darkness stealing over him. "Say it again."

I didn't care my dress was only half undone, I rolled onto my back, slipping beneath his inert hands. "Husband."

His gaze dropped to the front corset of my gown. "That word makes me hard."

The spaghetti straps slid off my shoulders, tickling my skin. "How hard?"

"So fucking hard."

"Show me."

He gulped. "Show you?"

I nodded, reaching for his tented slacks. "I want to see."

Darting out of my grip, he climbed off the bed, a slow burn building in his gaze. "*Why* do you want to see?"

Coyness slipped into my blood. He wanted to play? I could play.

Sitting up on my knees, I struggled against the imprisoning nature of the silk layers and licked my lips. "Because it's mine and I want to see what my marriage has bought me."

His hands fisted. "*Bought* you?"

"Uh huh." The conversation turned anchor-heavy with want, sinking through the yacht to the seabed below. I'd never been so needy, so ready for sex. I wanted him desperately, but at the same time, I loved the anticipation, the building joy that we could touch whenever we wanted but chose a little self-denial.

Jethro's hands flew to his belt. Never taking his eyes off me, he unbuckled the clasp, slipping the black leather from the loops. "If you get to see me, I want something in return."

"Oh?" My knickers grew shamefully wet. "What's that?"

Taking a step back, he crooked his finger. "Get off the bed."

Without a word, I obeyed.

My bare toes hit the soft carpet. My high heels had fallen off as Jethro carried me down the gangway to our room after leaving the party.

"Take your dress off." Jethro's left hand looped his belt tight around his fist while his right one disappeared into his black boxer-briefs.

The train of my dress resembled a wake of lace, the undone buttons giving me enough room to slink out of it and let the combined corset and overlay slip to the floor.

I stood before him in the sheer teddy I'd had Jasmine order for me online. She'd hidden it for me so it would be a surprise on our wedding night.

Tonight.

We're married.

The words sporadically kept popping into my head like toys on Christmas morning.

I'm a wife.

I have a husband.

There was nothing more erotic than that. Nothing more tantalising or desirous.

Grabbing his cock, Jethro swallowed hard. "Christ, you're beautiful."

The intensity in his eyes stripped me bare. I struggled to keep my hands by my side and not pluck at the garter belt attached to the unsubstantial G-string or run my prickling palms over the silky pantyhose.

I let Jethro drink me in because I had every intention of doing the same.

My eyes were selfish. My body greedy. My soul hungry.

"I want to bite every inch of you. I want to rip off your lingerie and take you hard. I want to bury you in my arms and never let you fucking go."

Jethro's voice mimicked a tidal wave on sand, velvet and soothing but rough and wild.

His hand worked harder, his quads tensing beneath his slacks. The action alone made my nipples throb with need.

"I can't stop staring at you." Jethro's jaw clenched as he stroked faster. "Nothing else matters knowing you're mine and

I can touch you, taste you, fuck you however I want."

The urge to touch him overwhelmed me. I wanted to consummate our marriage.

Now.

However, Jethro drove me to breaking point. The least I could do was return the favour. Drifting my hands from my throat to my breasts, I tweaked my nipples through the sheer teddy. "I love knowing you're mine. That your fingers belong inside me, your cock was made to pleasure me, your mouth designed to kiss me every day."

Jethro stumbled. "You have no idea. Every day, Nila. Every fucking day I'm going to give you those three things."

The room swam with lust, inviting the ocean below to transform air into liquid and oxygen into molten heat.

Dropping my hands to my pussy, I fingered myself through the lace. "I want to see you. I want to see your hard, long cock. I want to get on my knees and suck you. I want to feel you shatter and lick up every drop."

"Fucking hell." Jethro broke first.

My heart leapt with triumph as he stalked toward me, wrenched his hand from his trousers, and grabbed mine to replace it. His other hand latched around my nape, the buckle of his belt clinking against my collar. "Touch me, Needle. Fucking feel how much I want you."

My fingers instantly obeyed, stealing his invitation and invading his underwear. The moment my touch met velveteen steel, his stomach rippled with tension.

Grabbing a fistful of my hair, he growled, "I want your lips around my dick. I want your tongue lapping what I give you. But for now, now, I can't fucking think straight. I can't do this anymore. I need to be inside you. *Immediately.*"

His lips smashed against mine, his groan slipping deep into my chest. I battled his tongue, hints of violence and danger unravelled my decorum faster and faster.

The kiss turned fatal, killing off any last worries or maladies.

The ignition between us turned viperous as our past was suddenly deleted. The lid on our previous lifetimes snapped closed with finality. And a blank new page spread out before us. We were the quill and ink ready to pen a new chapter.

"Nila—" Jethro's touch turned savage, his tongue making mad love to mine with unscripted synchronicity. His touch became a Ferris wheel of caresses and demands, pushing me onto the bed again.

Splaying my hips, he stepped between my spread legs. The moment I rested on my back, he ripped at my knickers, yanking them down my legs. The garter belt fastenings pinged away, relinquishing the pantyhose and leaving me bare.

I couldn't breathe. I could barely stay within the boundaries of my skin as Jethro slammed to his knees and yanked me closer to his mouth.

His breath seduced me first, breezing over my clit, followed by filthy, delectable words. "I have no doubt we'll fight and make-up. We'll spend every day sharing a different experience, but this…this is the best part of today." His fingers danced over my entrance, teasing me with distraction. "I'm going to eat you, Needle. I'm going to lick and fuck you with my tongue before I fuck you as my wife."

His fingertips flew to my pantyhosed thighs, holding me down. "You're the sunbeam to my black diamond…"

My heart billowed at the poetic confession. "Jet—"

My hands dove into his hair, looping through the strands. He lived in my heartbeat, my breath, my thoughts. And now, he lived in my soul because we'd traded one for the other with our vows.

His tongue touched me first, a tentative lick—followed by the wet heat of his mouth. I bucked, my fingers clutching his hair for an anchor. Dizziness took me hostage; I didn't know if it was vertigo or Jethro's mastery.

He kissed my clit, moving to my entrance with a pointed tongue. The first quest inside me wrenched a moan from my chest. A very loud moan.

I craved more, more, *more.*

Tugging on his hair, I arched my hips, demanding what I needed.

Jethro chuckled, turning my world topsy turvy. "Not enough for you, greedy wife?"

His head ducked, his tongue pushing inside me...*deep* inside.

"Oh, God." My entire body contracted, begging for everything he wanted to give. The first ripple of an orgasm made me gasp. Yes. *Yes, yes, yes.*

"No, not yet." Jethro stopped, ending the ladder of bliss.

I growled, pushing my cheek into the bedding. "Tease."

He blew on my pussy, drying his saliva and activating a whole other world of enslavement.

"I don't want you coming. Not until you're screaming."

My eyes met his. "I'll scream. I'll do whatever you want."

He grinned. "I'll remember that next time you're arguing with me over some mundane thing."

"Our life will never be mundane."

His gaze clouded a little. "You're right. You've shackled yourself to a VEP."

Smiling, I stroked his bristled cheek. "Wrong, I shackled myself with a diamond heir who I share six-hundred-years of history with. That alone means our future will never be drab."

His head tilted in my hold, his glistening lips pressing against my palm. "You're right."

Tearing his face from my touch, his mouth landed back on my pussy. "Let's start rewriting history right now."

His tongue dived back inside me, tearing away comprehension.

I writhed as the promise of a release built quickly and sharp. A violent crackle of lust doused my system as his tongue thrust so deep, I convulsed on the covers.

Gone was the patience of making me wait. Gone were the threats of wanting to make me scream. It was no longer a threat but a promise.

He would make me scream—with or without my permission.

A release, as well as the sharpest cry, percolated in my heart like bubbling champagne ready to escape the bottle of my body.

"Will you scream?"

His tongue penetrated again, destroying every last wall and filling up every remaining crevice inside me. I became whole as his groans vibrated against my slippery flesh, the physicality of sex turning into an emotional reward the longer he licked.

Pleasure built and built and *built* as his rhythmic sucking destroyed me.

"Scream, Nila." Two fingers suddenly replaced his tongue, spearing deep, tearing my orgasm from eager into existence.

I had no choice.

I came.

And came.

And *came*.

Two fingers became three, twisting me open, dragging far more pleasure than I thought possible.

I rocked and thrashed and screamed.

I screamed for Jethro. For our future. For every day of our lives unwritten.

"Fuck." Jethro's five o'clock shadow sandpapered my inner thighs as he granted me such a delicious release. "Again."

Every inch of me burned and tingled. "There's no way."

Jethro took my denial as a challenge. "There is a way." He blew hot air over my swollen pussy. The warm breeze did nothing to temper raw and throbbing nerves.

My legs trembled to close. I wanted to rest. I *needed* to rest.

The tip of his tongue licked my folds, granting tenderness after a feral finishing. "You will come again. You'll come as many times as I command. After all, tonight is our wedding night, and I love watching you come apart. I love knowing I bring you pleasure. I love hearing you pant and moan. I love the way your cunt clutches my fingers as if afraid I'd ever leave you."

His three fingers slowly moved in and out of me, spreading my wetness, forcing my body to spindle into another climb.

He didn't rush me this time, taking every second and stretching them until my satedness gave way to hunger. The steady gathering made me breathless, my body tightening and quickening under his erotic conducting.

"Come for me."

My toes curled as he increased his pressure, but I wanted something more.

"I can't...I need—"

"What do you need?"

I rocked my hips, giving myself over to the creature he'd made me. "I need your cock. I need you riding me. I need to feel you claim me completely."

His teeth nipped my clit, a rumbling growl spilling from his mouth.

"I need you to come with me, Kite."

In an effortless move, he leapt from knees to feet. His cock was a javelin, proud and hard, while his slacks hung precariously on his hips.

His face set into a sexual scowl; his eyes demonic with need as his fingers grabbed my arse and arched my spine. His features set into stone, skin lashed over bone far too handsome for my heart. His golden eyes glowed with grey shadows, dilating with the need to break all boundaries, embrace every want and no longer limit himself with control.

He'd made me come. He'd ensured my body would accept his size with no hardship. He wouldn't hold back.

I didn't *want* him to hold back.

My mind segmented. Part of me paid attention to this incredible man about to fuck me and part turned animalistic. Spreading my legs, I welcomed him closer.

The bed jerked as his knees hit the edge. I went to scoot higher so he could climb on, but he stopped me, yanking my hips upward.

"No. Like this."

With gritted teeth, Jethro bent his knees, and in a seamless move, the tip of his cock found my drenched entrance.

My gaze riveted to his fully clothed body. The sheers of my pantyhose wrapped around his hips, the crumpled silk of his white shirt and the diamond pin glinting on his blazer.

Our eyes locked as he slipped inside me.

My mouth fell open as his immense length hit the top of me and stretched me wider than any finger.

I shivered; goosebumps sprouting as he sheathed himself balls deep. So possessing, he stole any remembrance of who I was.

Staring into his eyes, I knew he would take me hard and fast. My fingers clutched the sheets, preparing myself for how he would use me.

When he didn't move, I licked my lips, rocking my hips a little.

His head fell back, the tendons in his neck stark and tense. "Christ…"

"Fuck me, Kite." I moved again, enticing him to take. "I want you to fuck me."

Anticipation hovered like a curtain waiting to be shredded.

Temper swelled and I wrapped my legs tighter around his hips. "Fuck me, Jethro. Fuck me. Please, fuck—"

He didn't let me finish. Pulling out, he slammed back inside, penetrating in one fierce thrust.

I gasped as shooting stars arched out from where we joined. The connection was far too intense. Far too deep and demanding. He was so big, so hard, so *so* deep.

He'd taken me with everything. Nothing bared. I'd never felt him so open, so completely controlled but treasured at the same time.

Jethro's domination of my heart and body exploded my desire until I begged for another release. I needed another orgasm, and I needed it while we were both raw and wounded by love.

I clenched around him, proud and smug at having him inside me. He'd taken me, but I'd taken him. I held him in my body. I was his home.

His fingers switched to hands, holding my hips as he thrust again. And again. His strokes stretched nerve endings until the fluttering wings of another release begged to form.

His entire body hardened, his arms trembling, his suit whispering with every thrust.

Pulling out to the very tip, he rammed hard inside me. Over and over. Sweat decorated his forehead from being fully dressed as he let euphoria claim him.

His groan was primitive and so low; it slipped into my chest, wrapping around my heart. "Christ, you feel so incredible."

His hold tightened as his thrusts turned to fucking. The bed moved with his knees and my breasts bounced from his furious claiming. Every hot drive nailed me to the bed as he fell over me—turning from standing to squashing.

Having his body blanket mine, having his cock scatter my thoughts, turned me molten.

Pleasure rippled through me again and again. Keeping time with his fucking, pushing us up and up.

I gave myself over to ecstasy.

Harder.

Harder.

Long, invasive strokes.

Every second I came undone, losing my sense of self.

Burying his face in my neck, Jethro held me so tightly, he almost stopped my breathing. Our torsos glued together, but our bottom half worked harder, faster. We fucked each other to heaven.

"I've never been so hard." His lips found mine, his tongue driving into my mouth. "Never been so fucking deep."

He pounded into me, never breaking his pace.

I mewled and begged and said things I would never

remember.

I was helpless.

I was powerful.

I was desperate.

I was sated.

My orgasm switched into a storm, drenching me with raindrops, turning me into a river.

Holding my hair, his thrusting turned vicious. The crown of his cock stroked my inner walls, stretching my ache, coaxing my orgasm to teeter on the final pinnacle.

"Come, Nila." His teeth captured my bottom lip as he groaned long and low. His own orgasm started slow, thrusting inside me with calculated possession.

His back arched; the base of his cock rubbed my clit perfectly.

The first splash of his cum set me off.

I climaxed in one quick unravelling, wave after wave, milking him as he came. The release magnified as Jethro kept fucking, kept claiming.

His arms suffocated me, his body pinning me as his hips continued to pump until he spent every drop of his desire.

Minutes and heartbeats became uncountable as we lay there, hot and sticky but more in love than ever. His lips whispered over my jaw to my ear. "I married a goddess."

I chuckled. "No, you married a Weaver."

He nipped my lobe. "And now she's a Hawk." The flash of his grin stopped my heart, then like a defibrillator, restarted it in this new world he'd given me.

Rolling onto his side, we both winced as his cock slipped out, lying spent on his lower belly. Following him, I rested my head on his chest, letting the heavy *thud-thud* of his heartbeat rearrange my own.

My arms and legs quivered with residual pleasure, melting me boneless onto him. "Did we really just consummate our marriage?"

Jethro's arm banded around me. A kiss landed on the top

of my head. "I think fucking each other close to death is more the correct term."

Raising my eyes, I smiled. "Well, your destiny was always to kill me. If you do it by orgasm, I won't complain."

His eyes narrowed, filling with past debts and things I no longer wanted to think about. The love he held for me couldn't be denied as he gently kissed my lips. "My destiny might've been to kill you, but I've rewritten fate. Now, I'm going to do everything in my power to make you immortal."

My heart skipped at the passionate vow in his tone. "How will you do that?"

He nudged my nose with his. "By turning our duo into a family.

"By making you a mother."

Six Weeks Later

MARRIAGE WAS BETTER than any other gift, wealth, estate, or luck combined.

Being married to Nila made my life, my very fucking world, complete.

The past six weeks had been a chaotic mess of building new goals, guiding our dreams forward, and slipping into new patterns of normalcy.

Tex had found Jacqueline.

Nila and Vaughn had stared at the photo of their sister for days before deciding to set up a meeting.

They'd all agreed to meet somewhere neutral. A restaurant two weeks from now.

I feared how fraught everyone's emotions would be that night, but I would be beside her every step.

Not a day went by where I wasn't fucking awed by Nila. She handled her sister's reappearance, her new world, and my need for her emotional comfort with ease. She guarded my condition when we were out in public. She knew exactly how to treat me so I felt loved but not mothered.

And she let me do everything she did for me in return. She allowed me to provide a home for her, deliver gifts in both physical and emotional capacity.

Together, we'd found a new happiness, and I lived in its bubble every second of every day.

After our wedding and honeymoon in Santorini, Nila had returned to her craft with passion. She sewed late into the night while I completed ledgers and created new loyalties. We would often work side by side, sometimes in the Weaver quarters where all her fabric, supplies, and mess still lived; sometimes in the front parlour where I liked to drink up the sunshine, and sometimes in bed. A lazy afternoon where we stayed hunkered in warm covers and did the bare minimum of adult responsibilities so we could play beneath the sheets for the rest of the day.

And today, all that hard work had come to fruition.

My heart burst as roses spewed from all around us, kissing our feet.

Nila clung to my forearm, breathing hard, combating any vertigo spell she might endure.

I'd done my best to find a cure for her. I'd scoured website after website, consulted doctor after doctor. Some said it was an iron deficiency, so I stocked her up on vitamins and minerals. Some said the brain would eventually cease granting dizzy spells as it grew to equalize. However, seeing as she'd had it all her life, I didn't see that happening.

The best solution I'd found so far were a series of exercises called the Canalith technique. It helped, but hadn't fixed her.

But we had time, and I wouldn't stop trying.

For now, I would be her anchor, holding her close in a sea of tilting worlds.

"They adore you, Needle."

Her face met mine, painted with camera flashes. "They adore the collection. Not me."

I shook my head, looking over the carpet of journalists, photographers, and celebrities.

Fashionistas and reporters from all over the world had

come to witness Nila's Rainbow Diamond Collection. The collection she'd started when she'd stood naked on Hawksridge lawn about to run for her life through the forest.

She'd told me being naked that day and wearing only diamonds had given her the strength to run. It'd also been the inspiration to create her best showpieces and couture designs yet. Her brand, *Nila,* graced not just the high fashion world but shops and local department stores, too.

I'm so fucking proud of her.

Tonight, she hadn't shared the limelight with any boutique or label. The entire two-hour production had been piece after piece she'd created at Hawksridge and a few pieces she'd saved from Bonnie's wardrobe made courtesy of Emma and her ancestors. Those vintage pieces were heralded as a fashion comeback and the words 'Victorian lace' and 'crinoline skirts' wafted on the warm air inside the theatre.

"You did it. Be proud." I nuzzled into her neck. My teeth ached to bite, but I restrained myself. Tonight. Tonight, I would bite her and show her just how fucking proud I was.

"I couldn't have done it without you." She leaned into my embrace, bringing her scent of vanilla and orchid perfume.

"That's not true, but thank you all the same." I kissed her ear, careful not to disrupt the intricate up-do Jasmine had helped her with. The past few weeks had flown by and the shorter cut I'd given her in the stables had grown, thick and glossy—the perfect length to fist while her mouth fitted around my cock.

I hardened, remembering her swirling tongue last night.

We'd arrived two days ago in Milan—in the very same theatre where I'd stolen her all those months ago.

Time had its own strange irony.

I'd ended her life in this place.

And yet she'd come back to life here, too.

A year ago, I'd come to steal her from the limelight and prevent anyone from enjoying her creations. Now, I shared her with those who valued her skills and fought each other for the prestige of wearing her art.

All around us stood the models from tonight's show. The Rainbow Diamond collection truly was spectacular. Pastels, pinks, purples, teals, yellows—an array of fabrics Nila had educated me on and cuts and gathers and fancy needlepoint she'd explained every time she worked.

Standing beside her, I couldn't for the life of me remember a single stitch's name. All I could remember was how much I loved her and how stunning she was in a gown made of bewitching smoke.

Obviously, it wasn't smoke but silk and tulle and any number of materials she forced me to recall. But the panels of midnight down her tiny waist and the glitter of black beads down the front made her the crown of the show, the black diamond of her empire.

Every time she swished in front of me, I wanted to throw my tuxedo jacket over her shoulders to hide the scrumptious line of her spine and the swell of her arse below.

I appreciated the skill and design of the dress, but I didn't appreciate the way men gawked at my wife.

One of the boutique shops that'd already bid at auction and won Nila's new collection climbed on the stage and presented her with a bouquet of white roses. The dark-skinned man kissed her cheek, smiled at me, and faced the audience to reinvigorate the clapping.

For once, I didn't mind being in a crowd this size. Not because Nila was beside me and I'd become accustomed to tuning into her thoughts when in a gathering such as this, but because everyone had one focus: impressed awe.

Nila waved at the cameras, bowed—hiding the little wobble by digging her fingernails into my cuff—and turned to leave.

Not so fast.

I held her a second longer. I wanted to bask in the moment. I wanted to absorb every thought and feeling because tonight was special for Nila but special for me, too.

Tonight was my thirtieth birthday.

I'd made it.

Nila wasn't beheaded, her body wasn't rotting on the moor with her ancestors, and I wasn't dead at the hands of my father.

We'd turned evil into benevolence and lived a life worthy of deserving.

"Come on, it's time to go." She tugged on my hold, swaying in her stupidly high heels.

I cupped her elbow, turning her to face me. Unfortunately for her, she couldn't keep surprises and I knew tonight she'd already planned a birthday party for me. I didn't know where or what it would entail but I felt her excitement at surprising me and her enjoyment at celebrating such a huge milestone. A milestone we both feared would never come to pass.

However, there was something else, too.

Something she guarded and protected. Something that meant a great fucking deal to her and she hadn't told me.

For the past couple of weeks, I thought it was the collection. The fact she'd finished the entire wardrobe of twenty three dresses and other apparel was a huge feat.

But now…now, I knew it wasn't that because the secret still glowed bright inside her.

Nila looked once more at freedom, sensing my determination to make her tell me. I hadn't meant to trap her on the runway and force her to spill in front of the world of fashion. But where else was she the most vulnerable?

I held her up. I kept her imbalance at bay. The least she could do was—

"I have a secret and I can't keep it any longer." Nila sighed, fighting a smile. Camera flashes continued to go off along with the stray rose thrown as the models paraded one last time behind us.

I let out a breath. *About bloody time.* "I thought as much." Bending my knees, I stared directly into her eyes. "You've done a good job at hiding it from me."

I froze as she raised her hand, brushing aside my salt and pepper hair, showing the world the utmost affection between us. We were private in that respect. After the *Vanity Fair* article at our wedding, we avoided all mention and interviews.

I sucked in a breath as she cupped my neck, bringing me closer. "You haven't been able to guess?"

I shook my head, my hair mixing with hers. "No." I let myself dive deeper into her thoughts, searching for the answer to her hoarded truth. Her emotions were murky, mixed with bone-deep contentment and a sense of quiet achievement for all that she'd done tonight.

She swayed a little in my arms. "Is this truly the first time you can't guess? You don't know what I'm about to say?" Her lips pursed. "Because I already know you figured out my surprise about your birthday party tonight."

I laughed. My body relaxed, melting into her the more we spoke. I forgot where we were. I ignored the thousand other thoughts and human psyches. It was just us. Needle and me.

My wife.

"Instead of teasing, how about you put me out of my misery?"

Her eyes glittered, mimicking the diamonds around her throat. "I rather like having a secret for once. I think I might enjoy it a little longer."

I growled, wrapping my arm around her waist. The rustle of her skirts sounded loud over the murmur of the audience. "Tell me…. Otherwise, I'll have to use more forceful means the moment we're in private."

She licked her lips. "Promise?"

I rolled my eyes. "You're really going to drive me mad, huh? Fine, the moment I've blown out those bloody candles on whatever cake you bought—"

"I'm pregnant."

My mouth fell open.

Everything paused.

I couldn't move, speak, think.

Pregnant?

Fuck, she's…pregnant.

My mind scrambled, trying to make sense of the word. My heart bucked, squeezing every drop of oxygen from my lungs.

Nila chuckled at my lack of intellect. Her fingers looped with mine, pressing against her belly. "Pregnant, Kite. As in…I'm going to have your child."

My legs gave out.

I crashed to my knees on the stage in front of thousands of fucking people.

Tears shot to my eyes as I stared at her flat belly. The skirts and petticoats of her smoky gown hid any flutter or growth, but my heart sprang with knowledge. "You're—you're…" I couldn't finish.

The crowd went silent as I wrapped my arms around her legs and hugged her close. I kissed her stomach. I swore on everything I owned that I'd do whatever it took to be worthy of this new gift.

Pregnant.

She's pregnant.

I glanced up, drinking in her glowing face. "Ho—how?"

She curved over me, her eyes darting between me at her feet and the crowd. "Get up, they're all watching."

"I don't care. They can see what true love looks like. I'm not ashamed to worship you, especially after you tell me something as life changing as this." Pulling her down to me, she kneeled in her dress, eye to eye.

"How? I thought—"

She shook her head, smiling wide. "The contraceptive you gave me before the Third Debt wore off months ago. I meant to tell you I wasn't on birth control, but then I thought…we have everything we could ever need. We won over seemingly impossible odds. Why wait? We're young but wise. We've proven we know what's right and wrong."

Her hand cupped my cheek, shaking a little but so damn strong. "I want to have your children, Jethro. I hope you don't mind I made the decision for both of us."

"Mind? Why the fuck would I mind?" I crushed her to me, crumpling her feathers and rhinestones, messing up her elaborate hair with kisses. "This—it's more than I could ever ask for." Cupping her face, I kissed her deep.

I poured my heart and thankfulness down her throat.

"How—how long?"

She sighed, holding onto my wrists. "I'm not sure. A few weeks…possibly a month or so."

A stupid grin spread my face. "Do you know what it is yet?"

A girl.

Please, let it be a girl. Just like Nila.

A child I didn't have to worry about facing such horrendous debts. A firstborn daughter who would survive and not be made to pay for historic crimes.

She shrugged. "I don't know. But whatever it is, I know you'll love it and me, and we'll fill Hawksridge with the sounds of laughter."

I couldn't stop myself.

Clambering to my feet, I swooped her into my arms. The train of her dress rippled over my arm as I stood in the centre of the stage with so much fucking pride I could fly.

Glaring into the ever-invasive cameras, I announced, "My wife is pregnant."

The theatre erupted into applause.

I didn't care.

All I cared about was getting somewhere private so Nila and I could have our own celebration.

Turning my back on the world, fading out the claps and happy conversations, I kissed my wife. "I love you. I love you so fucking much."

Nila laid her head on my heart, making me wondrously complete. "I know."

Three Years Later...

"GOOD NIGHT, GOOD NIGHT, DON'T let the bed bugs bite."

The squeal echoed merrily around the room as Jethro blew raspberries on the belly of our child. Our firstborn. Part Weaver, part Hawk.

The past few years had gone by so fast. We became a true family—working together, loving together, learning and evolving and laughing.

My pregnancy had been easy. Thanks to my fitness from running, I remained supple and able to work until the day I delivered. Jethro would often find me in the Weaver quarters, sewing and sketching with my belly ballooning as the days stretched on.

He never told me to stop. He supported whatever I wanted to do. He held my hand when I walked the estate and commandeered the kitchen at all hours to concoct my ridiculous cravings.

He absolutely doted on me, and I fell deeper into love with him. I hadn't known there were so many layers to love. Sweet and sparkling then lusty and desiring, evolving into bone-deep and endless as the years slipped by. And the longer we lived together, the more we became soul-mates in every sense of the word.

He knew my thoughts without me verbalising.

I knew his concerns without him having to speak. We became in-tune with body language and heart-code…listening with more than just ears.

The further I progressed in my pregnancy, the more my father visited. His fear for my health grew until I resembled a blimp, soothing the scars of our past. He begged for the right to help decorate the nursery and almost singlehandedly bought London out of every nappy, cuddly toy, and cute baby clothes.

My twin was less impressed. He ribbed me constantly of the weight I'd gained—taunting me like a brother was allowed. On the nights he came to visit, he'd pat his washboard stomach and poke my humongous one, laughing good-naturedly. He even joked he'd buy me a few lessons with a personal trainer once I'd popped to get back into shape.

Jethro had not been happy. His eyes flashed with jealousy as Vaughn played up the angle of some beefed-up jock helping me stretch and train.

The night had ended with drinks for the boys and giggles for me.

I'd never been so contented.

And the day I'd given birth had once again changed my life. I'd been terrified—not that I told Jethro. My heart bucked and the fear of dying in labour stole all enjoyment of bringing life into the world.

But Jethro had been my prince, keeping me anchored, rubbing my back when vertigo struck and driving me calmly to the private hospital we'd arranged for the delivery.

The birth hadn't gone perfectly. I'd been in labour for twenty-four hours. The baby had turned the night before and faced the wrong way. An emergency caesarean had to take place after Jethro roared for the doctors to take away my pain.

For every one of my contractions, Jethro felt it. He sweated beside me. He trembled in sympathy. He almost threw up when the agony threatened to rip me apart.

But when the first screams of our child shredded the operating theatre, Jethro had slammed to his knees. His shoulders quaked in silent sobs as he let himself feel another conscience for the first time.

Not mine.

Not the doctors and nurses.

Our baby.

His.

Our son.

The moment the doctor cleaned up the newborn and swaddled him in Jethro's arms, he'd irrevocably changed. He became more than lord and master of Hawksridge. He became more than lover and friend.

He became a father. A protector. A single piece in a jigsaw of never-ending history. The look on his face when he stared into the eyes of his heir fisted my heart until I couldn't breathe.

It'd been the singular most awe-inspiring moment of my life.

And I'd done it to him.

We'd done it together.

We'd created the squalling new life wriggling in his embrace.

He'd found his peace.

His centre.

Our son cooed as I brushed his bronze-black curls off his cherub cheeks. To begin with, I'd been terrified of making a mistake—of being the worst mother imaginable. But once I returned home to the Hall, the cooks and cleaners all came to welcome their new inhabitant; granting snippets of their own experiences, and filling me with courage I could do this. I could raise this little person. I could teach him how to be moral and kind and wise. I'd been able to break the Debt Inheritance. I could raise a baby boy, no problem.

Jethro touched my hand from the other side of the cot, looping his pinkie with mine. Our son wriggled in his bed, grabbing our joint fingers and squeezing them tight.

My heart glowed as Jethro strained across the crib, kissing me softly. "I love what we've created."

I smiled. "I'm rather glad about that."

The chubby fingers around ours pinched, demanding more attention. "Okay, okay, demanding little thing." Jethro let me go, bending over to kiss his son one last time. "It's time to go to bed."

"No!"

"Yes."

The little boy shook his head, loving his favourite game.

I stood quietly, watching son and father interact. The name we'd chosen couldn't be more apt.

Kestrel.

Kestrel 'William' Hawk after Jethro's original ancestor and closest brother.

Jethro sighed dramatically. "If you don't go to sleep, you won't get to enjoy tomorrow."

"Yes. Tomarrooww."

I smothered my chuckle. Kes was beyond intelligent for his age. He'd learned to talk far earlier than normal, but his little accent cracked me up.

"No, if you don't go to sleep, there is no tomorrow." Jethro grinned, blowing another raspberry on Kes's neck. "Know why?"

Kes frowned as if the question was incredibly important. "No."

"Because if you don't sleep, tomorrow can't come because you're still in today. That's why we sleep, Kes. So today can pass and our dreams can conjure a new beginning. You don't want to ruin that tradition, do you?" Tucking the sheets tighter around him, he smiled. "After all, Mummy and I will be in the future, living tomorrow while you're stuck in the past living today. We're going to go to sleep. That means you should, too."

Kes suddenly froze, his inherited golden eyes latching onto

me. "True?"

"Very true." Pressing the button of his nose, I murmured, "Go to sleep, little one, so we can have a good day. We'll go riding. Would you like that?"

He yawned wide, finally letting tiredness take him.

"Good boy." Removing my hand from the cot, I moved quietly toward the door. Jethro remained, bending to give Kes another kiss. Patting his son's tiny chest, he checked the nightlight was secure and the baby monitor switched on and synced to his phone.

The little boy who looked exactly like his namesake with cheeky golden eyes and floppy dark bronze hair snuggled in his covers, already falling into dreams as his father sneaked across the room to me.

"You do know he manipulates us to drag out as many minutes before bedtime as possible, right?"

I laughed quietly; stepping into the corridor of our wing, I left the door open a crack. "Did you sense that or just parenting 101?"

His arm snaked around my waist. "A bit of both. If we're not careful, he'll have us completely wrapped around his little finger."

"Eh, I think that's already happened."

Leaving the nursery, we padded down the corridor of the bachelor wing. Not that it was the bachelor wing anymore. We'd transformed many of the rooms into playrooms, media rooms, and revamped the bedroom with soft whites and greys rather than overbearing brocade and maroon leather.

It'd been the only part of the house we'd renovated and removed the symbolism of Hawks on plasterwork and architraving. The rest of Hawksridge was a monument to architecture and history. It wouldn't be right to tear apart something so rich and detailed.

The thought of heading to bed to do more than sleep crossed my mind.

After Kestrel's birth, I'd returned to running. It wasn't a

chore. I ran for freedom, for peace. I ran because it was something I enjoyed. The baby weight came off, and I returned to designing gowns for my figure. The caesarean scar was just another mark on my body proving I'd lived a life and won. But unlike the many others scars I'd earned fighting an age-old debt, this one I wore proudly because it'd been given to me by the greatest gift I could imagine.

And soon, I would have another gift.

I had another secret.

A secret I'd managed to keep far longer than the first. Sneakily hiding my growing bump with excuses and masquerades. I'd kept my surprise hidden for two reasons. One, I wanted to see how long it would take Jethro to sense my news. I constantly expected him to suddenly drop the dishes or stop doing paperwork and announce what grew in my belly.

But ever since Kes had come into our lives, his condition had mellowed. He now had two of us who loved him unconditionally and didn't walk a razor blade of hypersensitivity—he didn't need to. All he needed to focus on was happy thoughts and contentment.

Before Kes was born, I'd catch him having a stressful day and try to soothe his condition by giving all the love I could share. I'd grant him sanctuary in our connection and hold him as long as he needed. Being in crowds was still too much for him. Dealing with company travel didn't often happen as his need for silence hadn't diminished.

At the start of our relationship, when he'd told me how much he would drain me, how much he would rely on my love for him, I hadn't fully understood the ramifications of what I'd agreed to.

But now I did and it was the least I could do.

He'd given me so much. On a daily basis, he gave me more of himself than I could ever ask for, and to be able to help cure him after a long day dealing with people granted me power and connection.

But our son.

Well…he was the true cure.

Jethro only had to hug Kes and the stress in his eyes would melt. The strain in his spine would vanish, and the need for simplistic silence came from holding the two-year-old in the tightest embrace.

Two years.

I couldn't believe we'd had Kestrel Hawk II in our lives for two years.

My mind returned to my secret, subtly stroking the growing bump.

The other reason why I'd kept it from him was I wanted the moment to be special. I wanted to whisper in his ear and give him a treasured present after he'd given me so much.

Spinning my black diamond engagement ring, I remembered Kes's first week at the Hall. Jethro had disappeared for a day, telling me to rest and all would be revealed upon his return.

I couldn't believe it when he returned with a foal.

Tears had spilled as he clutched the halter of such a delicate little pony and pranced him proudly through the Hall to Kestrel's nursery.

There, the adorable dapple grey colt stuck his nose through the bars of the cot, snuffling at the baby, building the first stone of an unshakable bond between horse and rider.

We'd agreed to call the foal Gus—labelling the colt with yet another name from the man who watched over us. It wasn't for a few weeks until I found out the origins of where Gus had been sourced.

Jethro had returned to the breeder who'd given his brother Moth—creating yet another circle of fate, buying pedigree from excellent stock.

My heart overflowed; I came to stop in the corridor.

Jethro raised his eyebrow. "You okay?"

"I want to tell you something."

He paused, his nostrils flaring. "Tell me what?"

"Not here. I want to go somewhere special. Just the two

of us."

He frowned. "You're scaring me. Tell me." His hands latched around my hips walking me backward to the wall. Pressing me against the fancy tapestries, his mouth latched on my throat. "Don't make me torture you to learn what you're hiding, wife."

I melted as his tongue and hot wetness of his mouth sent needful flurries through my core. "Perhaps a swim? I could tell you in the hot springs?" My mind filled with happy moments, splashing with Kes in the hot water and making slow love to Jethro once our son was in bed. The springs beneath Hawksridge had become a regular part of our lives. And I happened to know Jasmine took Vaughn down there a number of times to not only ease her atrophied muscles but also to indulge in…other things.

His lips kissed their way over my neck to my mouth. Tilting his hips, a rapidly hardening erection nudged my lower belly.

I moaned, accepting his invite.

His breathing quickened as his tongue danced with mine. Kissing me slowly, savagely, sweetly. The Hall swam, and my leg itched to hook over his thigh, hitch up my skirt, and welcome his body into mine.

Planting his hand by my head, he held himself over me. His voice trembled with lust. "I won't let you distract me. I want to know what you're hiding, and if you want it to be somewhere special…I have a better idea."

"Oh?"

Pushing off from the wall, he took my hand. "Yes. You want somewhere priceless. Let's go for a walk on the grounds. The very land we own and safeguard for our son. That's the most special I can think of."

I couldn't agree more.

Our fingers linked as we moved through the house, nodding at Black Diamond brothers and waving at Flaw as we crossed the foyer. It wasn't late, about nine p.m., but the summer sky teased with dusk. The sun had gone, cooling the outside temperature, but my ankle-length skirt and gypsy blouse would keep me warm enough for a small excursion.

Our footsteps disturbed gravel and leaves as we left the Hall and meandered down the driveway.

Passing the orchard, my mouth watered remembering the juicy fruit we'd picked the day before. Jasmine did her best to teach me how to have a green thumb like her, but I wasn't interested; not when I had baby clothes to sew.

It hadn't escaped my notice the way Jasmine held little Kes. She wanted one. We'd had a late-night conversation once about her getting pregnant with Vaughn.

For a long time—too long—she hadn't let Vaughn touch her. She couldn't get over her fear that someone could love her, no matter how stupid such a notion was. They'd been together for over two years, and she'd confided it took her almost a year just to allow him to sleep with her.

"Where are you taking me?" I asked as we left the driveway and cut into the woods. Together, we followed the path where we'd been for a run, skirting past the graves of my ancestors.

My heart clenched, recalling the day we'd tended to the awful moor and made it a better resting place. After discussing the graves with my father and brother, we all decided to leave them where they were buried. However, we re-blessed the ground, had new tombstones engraved, and ensured the hilltop only held good manifestations rather than ill will.

It was fitting that both Weavers and Hawks were buried on the estate and had followed through with legalities for a personal graveyard permit, so we were fully within the law. I didn't visit often, but had no intention of hiding any of our history from our children when the time came.

Including Jacqueline.

I'd begun to tell her about our shared lineage but hadn't gotten very far.

We'd met five times over the past two years.

To begin with it was awkward and confusing to stare at a stranger who'd shared a womb and birthday. But slowly, we turned from polite acquaintances to pleasant friends. We had plans to take Kes to see her next month up in Cornwall.

She didn't have children of her own and had only just married her long term partner, Joseph. She was my sister...but it would take time to become family.

"Somewhere special." Jethro smiled in the dark. "I thought we'd walk off dinner...that okay?"

"Of course, more than okay." My mind raced with how to tell him the news.

A snuffling sound came from the undergrowth. I froze, peering into the bush, searching for a hedgehog or badger.

Squirrel came bounding out of the undergrowth, weaving around Jethro's legs.

"Bolly, what the hell are you doing out of the kennels?" Jethro scowled. "How the devil did he get out?"

I grinned, dropping to my haunches to hug the dog. He'd adopted me on my first night at Hawksridge and was still my favourite of the foxhounds. Jethro no longer hunted, but every now and again, we would gallop across the estate with the baying dogs at our heels.

The dog yipped, coming to lick my hand. "He can come with us."

"We'll take him back to the stables afterward." Jethro snapped his fingers. The hound heeled obediently.

Silence fell as Jethro and I moved further into the woods. The moon only illuminated so much, but our eyes adjusted. Following an animal path, we popped out in a little clearing where a few ferns and foxglove bowed in sleep.

I turned to Jethro to tell him my news, but his mouth landed on mine, hushing everything I wanted to say.

"Would you play a game with me, Mrs. Hawk?"

I grinned, his skin silver in the moonlight. "A game? What sort of game?"

His teeth nipped their way to my ear. "A game to replace

bad memories with good."

We'd done that with every debt. The octagonal greenhouse had become a favourite place for kinky sex and the lake shed its stigma of the ducking stool and became a prized picnic spot. We'd rechristened Hawksridge Hall with so many happy memories over the past few years.

My heart raced. "You have me intrigued. Go on."

He chuckled. "Remember that first day? When you ran for your life to the boundary? I told you to run. That I would chase you. And when I found you...you gave me the best fucking blow-job of my life."

I shivered. "I remember."

"I want to chase you again, Nila."

My eyes widened at the naughty, delicious thought of what he would do to me when he caught me. "Naked or dressed?"

His eyes flashed. "Run while you're dressed. It won't stop me from claiming what's mine when I catch you."

I panted, backing away from his arms. Already breathless, I had no idea if I'd be able to run very far. Not that I wanted to. But the sheer thrill of running from the man I loved, knowing what he would do when he stopped me, sent my blood racing. "How much head start do I get?"

"A few minutes." He bent and grabbed Squirrel by the scruff. "I'll have my friend here to help me. Just like I did that day." His lips twisted into a sexy smirk. "I suggest you run fast, Needle. Otherwise, I'll have you on the ground and my cock between your legs before you've gone a few metres."

Swiping my hair into a ponytail, I secured it with an elastic. "Okay." My nipples ached, and I grew shamefully wet. Walking backward, I smiled coyly. "Bet I get farther than you think."

"I suggest you stop taunting me and start running..."

"Let's see who will win." Pirouetting, I took off. My ballet flats flew, hurtling me away from Jethro.

The intoxication of being able to play and laugh bubbled in my blood. The moment he caught me, he'd take me. And once he'd claimed what was rightfully his—what would *always* be his—I'd tell him my news.

Leaping over a fallen log, I darted through the undergrowth, not caring I crunched twigs or crashed through large leaves. He would find me. And I wanted him to.

True to his word, he gave me a few minutes head start before Squirrel's howl sounded on the night sky, signalling his chase.

I ducked and parried around trees and roots, doing my best to get far. But instead of fear, I sparked with laughter and love.

"Are you running? Because I'm chasing." Jethro's baritone whipped through bracken.

I ran faster, my hair tie coming loose and ebony strands cascading down my back as I tore through a small everglade and into dense woodland.

I hoped I'd get farther. But Squirrel found me first.

His paws thundered behind me, reminding me he'd ruined my hiding place up the tree that fateful day. Puffing, I ruffled the dog as he ran beside me. His tongue lolling and black eyes bright with excitement. "Even when you were being a traitor, you had my back, didn't you?"

Squirrel yipped. I'd never get used to calling him Bolly. That wasn't his name—not with the bristly tail he had.

Breathing hard, I entered another small clearing. This one had a few saplings straining for the sky. I went to dash forward, but a hand lassoed around my wrist, yanking me back.

"Caught you, little Weaver."

I shivered, my core clenching with need. "Unhand me, Mr. Hawk. Otherwise, I promise I'll make your life a living hell."

"Never." He backed me swiftly against a tree, slamming my wrists above my head and biting his way along my collarbone. "I've wanted to do this all day."

My breath turned into moans as his tongue licked its way down my throat, over my collar, to the dip between my breasts. "Do what?"

"This." Spinning me around, he pressed my front against

the tree and bent to gather my summery skirt. My skin goosebumped as the sound of his zipper coming undone sent wetness pooling.

"All day I've stared at you. I grew hard for you while you hugged our son. My mouth watered to lick you as you sipped wine at dinner."

My throat tightened as Jethro's hands skated down my body, following my contours, latching onto my hips.

"You're so fucking perfect."

My back arched in his hold. The hot steel of his erection nudged between my legs. "Open wider, pretty Weaver. I need you, and I need you hard."

I jolted with the thickest, quickest desire I'd ever felt. My feet spread as Jethro tugged my skirt up.

"Jethro..."

"Let me do this."

"I'd let you do anything."

"Christ."

Lifting one foot, I allowed him to yank down my knickers and stepped out of them, moaning as he wedged me against the tree again, thrusting his hips against my arse.

I struggled to get my hands free, reaching behind me to stroke his side. "I need...I need to touch you."

"No, you need to let me fuck you."

"Do it, then. Take me. I'm all yours."

"Shit, Nila." His hands shook as his fingers dug into my skin. "I'm going to take you. Right. Fucking. Now." Grabbing my hips, he slammed inside me.

"Oh, my God." My head shot back as Jethro's large length took possession of everything I was. He wasn't gentle. He wasn't kind. He was a man taking what he wanted.

I had no thought of the gift inside my womb. I had no thoughts at all but him inside me and the feral way we joined.

I'd never felt such bliss or baser desires. We were two animals fucking in the middle of a forest. All alone aside from the moon and stars.

Grabbing my wrists again, he held them above my head as his teeth clamped around my throat. He groaned, thrusting hard, impaling every inch inside me.

"Fuck, I love you." His voice poured more fuel onto the already blazing lust and my core fisted his length, begging for more, fearing how hard he would take me.

"Oh, God, it's so good. You feel..." My eyes snapped closed as he rode me. His pace was furious and brutal, the pleasure sharp and overwhelming. "Don't stop. *Please*, don't stop."

His breath slinked down my spine as he pulled away to fuck me harder. "I have no intention of stopping."

Angling my chin with demanding fingertips, his mouth landed on mine, sucking, slippery. His kiss stole whatever facets of humanity I had left, and I completely gave in to him. I gave myself to the wild wetness of his tongue. I moaned as he made love to my tongue while fucking my body.

His free hand waltzed over every curve, greedy and firm, twisting my nipples, grabbing my entire breast in his hold.

"You love this."

I nodded, gasping around our kiss. "So much."

"You love it when I take you nasty and rough."

"Yes."

"You love it when I take you tender and sweet."

"Yes."

"You love me."

"A thousand times, yes."

I cried out as his cock hit the top of me, heralding an orgasm to spindle and gather. My knees wobbled and the bark of the tree rasped my cheek. But I wouldn't change a thing. Not one goddamn thing.

The rhythmic strokes of his tongue matched the claiming strokes of his cock.

"Feel me, Nila. Feel my cock deep inside you."

My nipples ached as more wetness gushed around his penetration. "I do. I feel every inch."

"Feel how fucking hard I am. How much I fucking I love you."

I spread my legs wider, arching my back for more.

"Kite…"

"Think how much you love me now, when the last time you ran from me, you hated me."

His voice added another layer to my orgasm. I wanted him so much. I wanted to come, but I didn't want this to stop.

"Think about how much we've overcome to deserve what we have."

I loved him losing himself in me. My soul echoed with his need. My body begged for his release. I felt him everywhere—in the air, the tastes, the sounds, the very heart of me. He was more than man; he was heat and power and forever.

He'd given me a child. He'd saved me from the debts.

He'd made me more than just human. He'd made me immortal. Immortal in his love. Immortal in his passion.

"Fuck, Nila. Whatever you're thinking about. It's driving me to come."

"Then come."

"Not yet."

His pace turned frantic, our breathing mingling in echoing gasps. His hand landed on my nape, holding me in place as he drove harder, faster. We were locked completely in each other's spell—a bombardment of rapture.

"Please," I begged. "More."

"I'll give you more." His fingers shot down my front, landing on my clit.

I moaned as delicious shards of lightning crackled beneath his touch. I was a second away from detonation. A single breath from—

I came.

The lightning turned to a supernova, unspooling with the speed of light, exploding through my chest, heart, and soul. My entire body clenched and rippled, cradling me in euphoria.

"Goddammit." Jethro's forehead landed on my nape and

he lost himself completely.

His cock jerked in and out, his stomach hitting my spine with every thrust. His groan cascaded down my back as the first spurt of his release shot inside me.

I didn't move as he filled me, found pleasure in me. I trembled with satisfaction even though I still ached from my orgasm.

The moment his release ended, his hands roamed over my back, massaging kinks, showering me in a perfect blend of gratefulness and submission. He'd taken me dominantly, but he'd given me everything for safekeeping. That was real power. The stuff that came after sex.

He pulled out, breathing hard. The slick trickle of his cum marked my inner thighs.

Twisting in his arms, I smiled at the affection and awe in his eyes. We'd captured a miracle and lived in a fairy-tale.

"Come here." His voice was hoarse and deep. Curling his arms around me, he embraced me with all the love we shared. The sex had been furious, but this was the epitome of tenderness.

My breasts pressed against his chest as my arms looped his waist, deleting all space between us.

We held each other for a long time, regrouping from coming undone so spectacularly.

Pulling away, Jethro's eyes latched onto my mouth. "Thank you." Bowing his head, his lips tickled mine. "Kiss me, Nila."

Those two little words had become my absolute favourite. I kissed him.

The dance was hot and wet, an erotic fusion of past and present with a lick of unforgettable futures.

Once we felt more human and not as raw and exposed, Jethro let me go. Pulling a handkerchief from his pocket, he gently wiped his pleasure from my thighs and ducked to slip on my knickers.

I held onto his shoulder as he pulled the lace up my hips,

hiding my nakedness. Letting my skirt fall back into place, I couldn't tear my eyes from him as he tucked his still hard cock back into his jeans and buckled up.

Squirrel bounded from the undergrowth with perfect timing, almost as if he'd given us privacy. He yipped, wagging his tail as Jethro tossed him a stick to chase.

I smoothed down my clothing. "Now you've just ravaged your wife in the middle of the forest, do you want to know why I wanted to go somewhere special?"

His lips twitched. "Of course, I do—"

He froze, his forehead furrowed. "Oh, my God. You're—you're—"

I rolled my eyes. "Seriously, did your condition steal my secret? After all this time, you guess right before I tell you?" Stamping my foot with mock anger, I growled, "I can't surprise you with anything."

Jethro didn't move. "So you are…"

I beamed. "I am."

He charged forward. His hands—the ones that'd been so sexually demanding and rough now held me as if I was spun glass. "Nila…hell, I can't believe it. What did I ever do to deserve this?"

Holding his cheeks, I kissed him.

I kissed him for every day we'd been together and every day we had coming.

My heart overflowed with joy. "I'm pregnant, Jethro. And this time…it's a girl."

Jasmine

WHAT DO YOU say to a brother who was the cause of so much pain, but also so much happiness? What do you say to a life that gave so much, yet extracted so much in return? What do you say to a dead sibling, a deceased father, a slaughtered mother, a deranged grandmother?

What do you say to life*?*

Sitting in my favourite spot in the Hall, I smiled as Vaughn slapped Jethro on the back, coming in from checking on matters around the estate. They'd become closer as time went on, each learning different worlds and responsibilities, sharing Weaver and Hawk secrets.

I didn't have the answers to life's questions, and I didn't have the wisdom to use what we'd endured for greater good. All I knew was we'd *survived*. We'd been given a fresh start, a happy future, an unsullied second chance. And I was sick to fucking death of not grasping it completely.

Nila had taught me something. She'd brought Jethro to life and Vaughn had stolen my heart in return.

For a while, I fought it. I ignored his advances and betrayed my desire for him. I didn't believe he truly wanted something so broken. However, day by day, week by week, he'd shown me what a fool I was.

Yes, my legs had been stolen from me. Yes, I hated my loss and some days couldn't shed my self-pity.

But now…now, I was stronger, smarter, and more adult

than child. Yes, I couldn't run. Yes, I couldn't stand or dance or skip. But who cared when I could kiss and love and hug and exist? Exist in a far superior world than most, enjoy far more enjoyable experiences than most, and adore far more deeply than most because I knew what it was like to lose.

I was lucky.

So terribly, terribly lucky.

We all were.

Life was far too short. History had taught me that. And Vaughn had given me the strength to be brave and embrace it—hardships and all.

I loved my family—both alive and dead, both evil and kind. I loved my lineage—both revengeful debts and righteous ending. I wasn't ashamed of my bloodline, but I had full intentions to make my future mean something. I wanted to dabble in charities. I wanted to give back what we'd taken. I wanted to make a *difference* with my life.

It was time to embrace every heartbeat because each was numbered, each was accounted for, and each was wasted by being fearful.

I'm no longer fearful.

I was sister to a lord. A powerful mistress in her own right. And matriarch to a six-hundred-year-old estate.

I had the means to make a difference.

I would never take life for granted.

And Hawksridge Hall would guard over all of us…just like it had for centuries.

Jethro

Five and a half years later...

"HAPPY BIRTHDAY TO you. Happy birthday to you!" Emma clapped her hands, wriggling in her chair to blow out the candles. "Stop singing! Now. I wanna blow now!"

Clamping hands on her tiny shoulders, I held her squirmy form in place. "So impatient."

Nila smiled, snapping the happy moment with the camera. The same camera Tex bought us for our wedding anniversary last year. At the time, I was grateful but not overly-excited.

In my world, photos and videos had been a reminder of bad things. I'd prefer not to catalogue such recollections. However, that was before I thumbed through a stack of prints Nila had taken of me playing unaware with Kes and the foxhounds one afternoon.

I'd frozen. So sure the man she'd captured was a total stranger. I didn't see the guy in the mirror staring back every day when I shaved. I looked upon a man who knew his place, *loved* his place, and was happy. *Truly* happy.

My heart glowed as my wife clicked and imprisoned special portraits of Emma's fifth birthday. That camera— something so small and simple—had become so precious, capturing irreplaceable memories, colouring moments of treasured time.

In my spare time—not that I had much between running the Hawk empire and raising two demanding children—I dabbled in film exposure. I'd transformed one of the many parlours in the Hall into a dark room. I preferred the old-fashioned way of developing. I got to touch the faces of my children, be the first to witness my wife's stunning smiling lips as the chemicals morphed her from nothing, to black and white, to vibrant colour.

Almost like how she'd brought me to life with her love, breaking me free from my self-imposed prison and granting magical pigment to my world.

Kestrel grabbed the edge of the table, throwing his head back dramatically for the birthday song. "Happy birthday to Velcro Smells. Happy birthday to you!"

I rolled my eyes as Nila bopped him on the head. "Don't call your sister that."

Kes rubbed his tussled hair. "What? She does."

"I do not." Emma stuck her tongue out. "You smell. You stink like, like, like...a *hedgehog.*"

Nila bit her lip so she didn't laugh.

I couldn't stop myself. My eyes met Jasmine's, and she burst into giggles. "A hedgehog? What the hell?" My sister looked at my wife. "Where have you been letting them play? I had no idea hedgehogs even had a smell?"

Vaughn bent over, coming back from the kitchen where he'd pilfered a few of last year's brew. This mix wasn't thistle and elderberry like at my father's birthday so many years ago, but lavender and honeysuckle. The liquor was strong, but I doubted I'd ever grow a palate where I would crave it. I preferred the expensive cache of cognac we had in the cellar. Not that I needed alcohol to be happy.

Thanks to Nila and my children, I lived in a state of bliss. Even when Kestrel and Emma were cranky and tangled with childhood emotions, I still basked in their love. I learned how to let my condition have full control of me because I had nothing to fear by soaking up the feelings of my beloved family.

Nila put down the camera and came to stand beside me. Her hand landed on her daughter's fuzzy black hair. Her face tilted toward mine, and we shared a brief kiss. Her eyes shot a silent message. *I'm having you the moment it's appropriate.*

My gaze hooded. *I'm having you regardless of appropriate time or not. The minute this cake is cut, you're mine.*

She sucked in a breath.

Forcing myself to look away and remain tethered to the room full of people, I smiled at the family and friends celebrating Emma's birthday. It drained me—so many people in one space all at once—but the afternoon of medieval games with jousting, dress-up, bouncy castles, and even a re-enacted sword fight had been worth the emotional strain. All day we'd had a child's dream out on the front lawn with water pistols and a petting zoo—combining old-world charm with modern simplicity.

Emma and Kestrel had explored every secret I'd set up for them and my chest warmed with pride to think I'd given them more than a childhood day of fun—I'd given them a happy childhood, and that was immeasurably priceless.

Merged voices rose together, singing the final line of the song. "Happy birthday to you!"

The burly men of the Black Diamonds—the ones vetted, vouched, and commanded by Flaw all clapped and cheered. V hipped and hoorayed, waving his arms and stealing a giggle from Emma while Tex shoved the five candle cake closer toward my daughter.

Five years old.

Fuck, time flies fast.

My heart twinged like it always did on big occasions. Small occasions, too. Every moment when I stopped and took the time to wonder how I got so fucking lucky. In those same seconds, I often thought of Kes. I remembered my brother, I missed our friendship, and I ached to share what I'd been given.

The guilt of his death still coagulated my heart. He shouldn't have died. If anyone deserved to survive during the massive purge of evil in my family, it was him. Nila knew how I felt, how I struggled to be deserving that I lived and he didn't. She helped me accept it. And time helped soothe it.

Kes might not be with us physically, but sometimes, I'd get a sense of his quiet humour as I wandered around the Hall. I liked to believe a part of him remained with us, watching over us until our time came to join him.

"Make a wish." Nila bent over, holding Emma's hair from catching fire as she jumped up in her chair and puffed her tiny cheeks. The little hellion planted her hands on the table, about to face plant into the pale pink icing of the castle cake.

"Wait." Nila shook her head. "Before you blow, did you make a wish?"

My ears pricked. I wanted to know what my daughter wished for so I could make it come true. My entire existence was to make sure every desire materialized. Within reason, of course. I wouldn't raise a spoiled brat.

Emma pouted, her eyes locked on the cake. "I made one already." She bounced in her frilly pink tutu. "*Please*, can I blow? I wanna blow. I made a wish. This is taking *forever*. I want cake!"

Kes laughed. "She's crazy."

I pinched his arm. "Don't call your sister crazy."

He slapped my hand playfully. "Whatever. You're crazy. Mums crazy. We're all crazy."

Well, I couldn't really argue with his logic.

"*Muuuumm!*" Emma squealed. "Let me blow!"

Nila laughed, letting her go. "Go on then, make sure you blow all five out at once. Otherwise, your wish won't come true."

Emma froze, soaking in that vital piece of information. She glared at the cake as if she'd wage war on the frosting rather than eat it.

She's so damn fierce.

I smiled.

She took after her mother.

Nila's black eyes met mine. She whispered under her breath, "Do you think she wished for a prince, a pony, or one of those silly flying fairies she saw last week at the store?"

I wrapped my arms around her middle, pulling her back to my front. I kissed the soft skin of her throat above the diamond collar. "I don't care. I'll make sure she has every one."

Her heart thudded against mine. "Even the prince?"

I reared back. "Hell, no. As far as I'm concerned, she's the next Rapunzel. Hawksridge has plenty of towers to keep her in."

Nila giggled. "Good luck with that. She'll just scale it and run."

"Run?" I nuzzled the back of her ear. Two words never failed to get a rise out of me. Run and Kiss. 'Run' because it reminded me of Nila being brave enough to try and escape, and 'kiss' because it was the moment she broke me and made me hers.

Emma had inherited her mother's bravery and exceeded even her brother in tree climbing acrobatics. I didn't know where she got the skill, but she loved being in the treetops more than on the ground.

A sudden memory of Nila hiding naked in the trees filled my mind. Blood siphoned through my body, swelling my cock. I subtly pressed my hips into her arse. "Talking of trees and running..."

She tensed then melted. Her arm looped up and behind her to secure around my neck. "If you bring a plaid blanket, I'll make sure to give you what I gave you then."

Kissing her cheek, I breathed, "Done." Lowering my voice even more, I whispered, "You really have to stop using those words. It's highly inappropriate that I'm hard at my daughter's birthday party."

Nila swivelled in my arms, planting her mouth to mine. Her lips fed me kisses as well as barely audible conversation. "You really have to stop making me love you so damn much." Her eyes met mine. "Can you feel it? How overflowing I am? How I don't know how to contain it tonight? I just...I need you."

The rest of the room faded—the world always did when Nila touched me.

"I do. I feel it."

She cocked her head. "What does it feel like?"

I glanced at Emma, who still hadn't decided how to blow all the candles out at once. "It feels like slipping into the hot springs beneath the Hall. Warmth and contentment lapping around me with a slight edge of pain from being too hot. But, unlike the hot springs, I don't have the discomfort of knowing I'll have to climb back into the cold and leave the warmth behind. You give it to me constantly."

Nila kissed my cheek. "You'll never be cold again." The double meaning of her words—that I would never be unloved again—throbbed.

Clearing my throat, I pushed her away and invited the room back into my attention. "Keep saying things like that and we won't see the rest of the party."

Nila half-laughed, half-scowled. "I'm torn in which I want more." Turning, she faced the table and Emma.

Kes rolled his eyes, never looking away from his sister, waiting impatiently for dessert. "Come on already."

"Pushy." Emma grinned, puffing out her little cheeks. Her lungs expanded and she blew raspberries rather than air but managed to get the flames to turn into curling spirals of smoke.

The room erupted into claps and cheers.

Emma didn't acknowledge the bikers or billionaires, secure in her place within their adoration. However, she did squeal and dance uncoordinatedly on her chair.

Nila grabbed Emma's tutu, just in case she toppled over. "Good girl. I have no doubt all your wishes will come true."

Kes stood by, his mouth watering. He didn't care his sister's spit just ended up all over the cake with her blowing attempt. All he wanted was sugar. Kid turned high as a damn kite whenever he had sweets. In that respect, he didn't remind me of his namesake. My brother had never truly let himself go—never been crazy or adolescently stupid.

At the time, I thought it was just him, but now, I think he did it for me. If he'd let himself get carried away, I wouldn't have had any choice but to be carried away, too.

Letting Nila go, I slipped my hand into my back pocket and squeezed the hidden box. Nila had seen this gift, but Emma hadn't. It would be the last present but the most valuable.

All day Emma had gratefully accepted gifts. I loved that she genuinely appreciated everything—from socks and sherbet to a new swing-set and pony. Her young emotions filled my heart to bursting, and in an odd way, I was able to relive my childhood through her, replacing unhappy times with excellent ones.

"Down. Down. I want to get down." Emma pointed at the floor.

Nila calmly plucked Emma from the chair, placing her on the travertine. "Don't go anywhere. I believe Daddy has a present for you while I cut the cake."

Nila's black eyes met mine. We'd been together for such a short amount of years, yet it felt like she'd been mine for eternity. I would never grow sick of waking with her in my bed, or sharing my breakfast with her by my side, or helping her sew late at night even though her needles drew more of my blood than I liked.

I love you.

She beamed. *I know.*

Tearing my gaze from hers, I dropped to my haunches and motioned Emma to come closer. It was surreal to protect and raise children named after two people who had meant the world to us; two people who'd died in the war between our houses. Kestrel had adopted some of my brother's quirks, but not all, and Emma doted on Textile in a way that made me wonder if she suffered a little of my condition.

There was no avoiding the avalanche of love and underlying despair from Tex that his wife wasn't there to see her grandchildren grow. Emma would hold his hand and sit quietly on his lap, plastering up his hurt with quiet affection.

Taking my daughter's hand, I looked toward the outskirts of the room. My sister-in-law, Jacqueline, lingered in the background. She'd come for a few days to celebrate Emma's birthday but couldn't shake the wariness the Hall invoked in her. Hawksridge had not been kind to the Weavers, and she hadn't accepted her lineage that easily.

Nila and Vaughn had gone out of their way to welcome Jacqueline into their midst, but she'd been raised differently. She'd been a single child in a stuck-up family. She didn't know how to handle large gatherings—and in that respect, I could relate.

We had happier times when we visited her in Cornwall— where Jacquie lived with her husband. There, on her own turf, her emotions were relaxed and confident while she lavished her little niece and nephew with love and antidotes.

She was a good aunt. However, her spiky black hair couldn't be any different to Nila's river of ebony. She shared the same eyes, same figure, same liquid grace, though.

Nila and Vaughn grew up believing they were twins; to find out they were triplets had taken some getting used to. However, the underlying history and mystery kept a moat from forming an intricate bond just yet.

In time, it would form. Nila would eventually warm her sister and help her dispel the remorse that she wasn't there to help. Shame was a powerful thing and Jacqueline couldn't shake the regret that she'd been firstborn by a few minutes, yet she hadn't paid the debt.

She didn't even fully understand the ramifications of the debt. Didn't care to dive too deep into history.

My heart thundered. If Jacqueline hadn't been secreted away and hidden, she would've been mine, not Nila. And the end to the Debt Inheritance might've been completely different, because even though I tolerated Jacqueline, I didn't connect with her. Her emotions were scatty and undeveloped compared to her sister. She would never have had the power to reach into my ice and shatter me from its hold.

My arms itched to hug Nila again. To thank her. To love her for being her.

So I did.

Straightening from my crouch, I quickly embraced my wife before dropping back to my haunches in front of Emma.

Nila accepted my hug with a soft smile, almost as if she'd followed my thoughts.

Emma smelled of cheese puffs and sausage rolls from the special treat for her birthday dinner. "Did you enjoy riding Hocus Pocus today?"

Emma clapped her hands. "I did. She's amazing. Can I go again? Right now?"

I swam in her infectious energy. "Not tonight. Tomorrow. We'll all go for a ride over the chase."

"Can we bring the birds? And the hounds? And Nemo?"

"Nemo?"

Emma looked at Nila. "You said you'd ask, Mummy."

Nila rolled her eyes affectionately. "Nemo is Emma's name for a kitten we saw advertised in the village. I told her we had more than enough pets." Ruffling her hair, she smiled. "You just got a pony. That's enough animal presents."

Emma pouted. I tensed against childish demands, but she balanced her emotions with such maturity, that pride washed through me.

"I know. Hocus is amazing." Leaning in, she pecked my cheek. "Thank you, Daddy."

My heart shattered with love.

It'd taken almost a year to source the perfect foal for Emma. I'd ordered a filly from the breeder who'd given me the colt for Kes.

At almost eight years old, Kes had become a proficient rider and rode with me daily, trotting beside me, cantering with courage, exploring the borders of Hawksridge as I taught him the value of land and heritage. Now, Emma could join us on her midnight filly called Hocus Pocus.

Letting Emma's sticky hands go, I reached into my back pocket for the box. Passing it to her, the room quieted as I kissed her soft cheek. "This will mean more to you when you're older, but I wanted you to have it now. Promise me you'll take great care of it and never lose it."

Her black hair bobbed as she nodded furiously. "I promise."

I laughed softly as she grabbed the red box and cracked it open. She had enough experience opening jewellery boxes. One of her favourite places was Diamond Alley and raiding Nila's precious collection. She said she wanted her mother's collar— even tried to pry it off one day with a nail file. Little did she know that it would've been on her little neck if she'd been born to another man in another time with the Debt Inheritance still in affect.

She was a Weaver girl. But now that name didn't come with such a curse.

Her little mouth parted as she took in the black diamond necklace I'd shown Nila the day I officially asked her to marry me.

Nila caught my gaze, twirling her engagement ring, letting me know her thoughts were with mine. She didn't need my condition to understand me—that came from unconditional love and a lifetime of listening to each other.

Helping Emma remove the chain from inside the box, I dangled the teardrop in front of her. "This is very special. Do you recognise the stone?"

"Yes." Her black hair bounced.

I'd never met a brighter child. She could memorize and recite diamond cuts and their flaws and attributes. She'd learned a few words in Swahili last time we were in Africa and even given the kids at kindergarten clothing advice from watching Nila effortlessly pin and style simple calico into a glorious gown.

She was a perfect blend of both of us. A magical piece of Nila and me.

"Where did you see the stone?"

She pointed at Nila's left hand. "Mummy's ring and bracelet."

"That's right. And now you have one, too."

"Because you love me as much as her?"

I laughed, gathering her in a hug. Kestrel moved in grabbing distance and I squeezed him in a group hug. "Because I love both of you as much as her. I love you all."

Nila subtly wiped sudden dampness from her cheeks, busying herself with cutting the cake. Jaz rolled closer, helping stack paper plates and take those full with pink frosting to a few of the Black Diamond brothers and family.

Once the room had received their piece of confectionary, Jaz wheeled toward me and handed out the plates of cake on her lap to my children.

Pinching Emma's nose, she said, "Now the present giving has ended, how about some cake? I want to eat your wish, little Velcro, so I can make sure it comes true."

Kes slung his arm over his sister. With boyish fingers, he grabbed the icing and smeared a huge handful into his mouth. "About time."

The room laughed.

And my world was perfect.

I was drunk.

Not on liquor or intoxicating substances but on happiness. Pure, unadulterated happiness.

Such a cliché expression: *I'm drunk on happiness.* But for the first time in my life, I could positively say it was true.

"Hey, man, we're gonna push off." Vaughn clasped my shoulder, squeezing tight.

The last few hours had passed in good company and gentle conversation. The crowded parlour had dispersed after the cake had been devoured and Tex and Jacqueline had gone to their guest rooms while Nila and I retired to the newly decorated den with the children. Jaz and Vaughn had joined us, pulling out Twister and other silly games to tire Kes and Emma.

"You're safe to drive? You guys can just crash here." I smirked. "It's not like we don't have the room."

Jaz smoothed the blanket over her legs, reclining beside Nila. "V has the clothing line reveal tomorrow. We want to get back tonight." Her eyes landed on Vaughn. The intimacy and tenderness between them layered my happiness.

I never thought my sister would leave Hawksridge, let alone find love and support her chosen partner in the limelight, where her disability was questioned and discussed. But she had and she'd never looked better.

The fireplace crackled warmly, the burgundy drapes ensconced us away from the rest of the world, and the scattered bean-bags and toys on the floor painted Hawksridge in a completely different light than the one that'd existed for so long.

"Do you need any final adjustments?" Nila asked, running her fingertips casually through Emma's hair.

My daughter's energy level dwindled. She remained awake, playing Legos with Kestrel, but the long day finally sneaked closer to sending her into slumber.

Vaughn waved dismissively. "Nah, I'm fine. You've given me enough of your time making the men collection perfect."

Nila glowed. "Anything for you."

Vaughn beamed. "Ditto, sis."

Over the past eight years, V and I became fast friends. He was prickly and opinionated, smug and sometimes arrogant, but he adored his twin and was besotted with my sister. He adored the ground Jasmine wheeled over and treated her with the utmost care and respect.

His friendship soothed the hole left behind by Kes, giving me the comradery to share a beer at a local pub or just discuss meaningless things, but he'd never be able to fill the emotional void left by my brother—nor did I want him to.

I enjoyed V's company, but he didn't control his thoughts around me like Kes could. I knew far more than I needed to about how much he loved Jasmine, how much he found the power in her forearms from wheeling herself around a turn on, and how much he longed to cradle her in his arms after a long day at the Weaver factory.

I shifted in my wingback, nursing the small amount of cognac I'd poured. "Well, I wish you the best of luck for the reveal."

"Thanks."

Taking a sip of amber fire, I asked, "You up for clay shooting next weekend?"

V rubbed his hands together. "Damn right, I am. Gonna kick your arse after the last beating you gave me."

"Come up for the weekend." Nila ran a hand through her long hair, loosely draping the strands over her shoulders. She'd slipped into a knitted jumper, and her hair weaved with the wool. I loved that the length was the same as the day I claimed her.

Jasmine smiled. "Sure. Sounds good. We'll come up on Friday and spend a few days with you guys."

"Sounds like a plan." Glancing at Vaughn, I pointed a finger. "However, if you're up here to shoot clay and play with your niece and nephew, then no sleeping in until midday."

Jasmine swallowed a laugh.

V simpered. "Hey, blame that on your sister. She likes mornings and things that happen in the *morning*."

Nila clamped hands over Emma's ears while Kes looked up with a confused glance. "V!"

He laughed, shrugging. "What? I won't get blamed for

sleeping in when it's not my fault."

I tossed back the rest of my drink. "Gross. I don't want to hear thank you very much."

V chuckled louder, ducking to slug my bicep. "Figured you'd knocked up my sister, might as well try to return the favour."

I choked on a mouthful of cognac. "Excuse me?"

His eyes gleamed as he glanced across the room at Nila and Jasmine, sitting side by side on matching bean-bags. Jaz used her chair, but V had become her legs. He seemed to know when she wanted to move, lifting her effortlessly from her chair and placing her wherever she wanted. Sometimes, he'd just randomly pluck her from wherever she was and march out of the room, only to return thirty minutes later with wind-pinched cheeks and swollen lips.

As much as I ribbed Vaughn for stealing my sister, I couldn't be more grateful. He'd given her a new life. He'd expanded her walls, given her a fresh world, and I'd never seen her so happy.

In summer, she had a tan from V pushing her through sunshine fields and carrying her to nap in the orchard. In winter, she sported a red nose—the only thing exposed seeing as V went out of his way to bundle her up so tightly.

For someone who'd never left the Hall, she now travelled with him on buying trips for his company, laughed more, and lived her life rather than just existed.

Vaughn looked at the picture-perfect scene before us. His joking switched to solemn want. "You have rugrats. Wouldn't it make sense for them to have cousins to grow up with?"

I frowned. They'd taken a long time to make that decision and I didn't think it was from lack of wanting children but Vaughn's fear that Jasmine wouldn't cope being pregnant.

I tried to block out the prying ability of my condition, but kids had been on their minds for a while. They'd either figured out the issues causing them grief or had finally decided to let nature take its course.

Nila looked up, making eye contact with me across the room. The rugrats V mentioned sat in front of her and Jaz. Two black and bronze-haired demons I wouldn't change in the slightest. The thought of filling the ancient Hall with laughter instead of tears was a perfect goal.

Clinking my empty glass with Vaughn's knuckles, I smiled happily. "Deal. Make Kes and Emma a few cousins but first...marry my damn sister and make an honest woman out of her."

V laughed. "Believe me, I've been trying. She accepted my ring but won't set a date."

I caught Jaz's eyes. I knew why. She tried to hide it, but her thoughts were always broadcast on a loud frequency. She didn't set a date because deep inside, she still didn't feel deserving of Vaughn when she wasn't 'complete.'

I didn't care I would sound stupid and let on just how many secrets I harboured, I whispered, "Jaz, you *are* complete. You're more than any other woman I know besides my wife."

She sucked in a breath, her eyes glittering with flames from the fire. "Thanks, Kite."

Vaughn paused, letting the random sentences fade before joking, "Besides, are you sure you want a Hawk to become a Weaver? What happens if some tyrant tries to claim our firstborn Weaver daughter in a few years?"

My heart panged, watching Nila and loving her so much it hurt. "They wouldn't take yours. They'd come after mine. I was the one who was supposed to change his last name, remember? But I didn't and the curse is broken. It's finished. Done. Over."

Vaughn sighed. "My mum would be proud of you, you know? Proud of how you stopped it and saved Nila."

I remembered Emma and her iron-gentle spirit. I'd grown to care for her during her short stay and looked up to her for how strong she was. "I should've saved her."

"We all agreed not to live in the past, remember?" Stepping away from me, Vaughn headed toward the women and two little ones by the fire. "We have a new future to enjoy."

Without conscious thought, I stood and followed him. Nila smiled as I stood over her, looking down at the two dark heads of our children. Her fingers wrapped around my bare ankle. "I missed you."

My heart swelled and cracked, pouring with adoration and contentment. "I missed you, too."

Dropping to my haunches, I positioned myself beside her and dragged her from the bean-bag and into my lap. Nuzzling her neck, I kissed her diamond collar and then her petal-soft skin.

She moaned under her breath, "I think it's bedtime...don't you?"

My eyes dived into hers, telling her without words that I needed her so goddamn much.

A small hand tugged on my jeans. "Daddy, story?"

I sighed. So much for bedtime.

I rolled my eyes dramatically. "And why do you think you deserve a tale, tiny Emma?"

Nila reached out and tickled the little girl who looked exactly like her. Same cheekbones, chin, and lips. However, Emma had my eyes—Hawk eyes—a trait so strong every single sibling of mine shared. "Where are your manners, Velcro?"

Emma giggled at Nila's nickname for her. On her second birthday, she'd fallen into a basket of Velcro teeth ready for invisible zippers. Her soft cotton jumpsuit latched onto the plastic thorns, ensuring untangling her took a lot of tugging and cursing. The damn child now had an addiction to pulling apart Velcro; she loved the noise.

Kestrel abandoned his Legos, shuffling closer to lean against my thigh. "Can we have a story? Just one. *Please?*"

I couldn't help myself. Looping an arm around his small shoulders, I hugged him. Nila on my lap and Kes and Emma wedged against my sides—what could be more perfect? "You want a story?"

Emma bounced up and down, but Kes merely nodded.

His thoughts sweet, steadfast, and protective. He adored his little sister. And if she wanted a story, he would make sure she got a story.

His golden eyes locked with mine, pleading. Goosebumps darted down my arms, wondering, if in some small way, my brother and best friend might've found a way to communicate via my son.

Kes wriggled in my embrace. "Tell us a story. Just one. Then bed. Promise."

Nila laughed. "How often have we heard that?"

Kes smirked, a lock of hair curling on his forehead. "Promise. Hope to die. Cross my heart."

Jasmine giggled. "Got that back to front, Kessy."

Kes stuck out this tongue. "Daddy knows what I mean."

I laughed softly as Vaughn slid to the carpet, resting his back against the chaise and scooping Jasmine into his lap. "You're right. I do know what you mean."

Kes clapped his hands. "Good. Gimme the story then."

"Story! Story!" Emma curled up, cocooning all of us in a family bubble.

This right here.

This was happiness.

And I was no longer drunk on it.

I was *infested* by it.

This was my family.

My new chosen family.

We won.

Nila's thoughts washed over me in an influx of honey and serenity. Her heart swelled with love.

Squashing my two children, I grabbed my wife and kissed her hard.

Kes pretended to vomit, and Emma squealed. Jasmine and Vaughn just groaned, "Get a room."

Nila broke the kiss, her onyx eyes glowing with tenderness. "I guess we owe these demons a story."

"I guess we do."

"I've got a story." Vaughn tickled Kes. "A story about a dragon and a little boy who got gobbled up."

"No!" Kes struggled, scrunching up his face and trying not to laugh. "I like Daddy's stories."

My eyebrows rose. "My stories?"

I didn't understand. Nila was the story queen. She'd trawl the internet for every Disney animation, picture book, and tale she could find. I'd just linger in the dark, listening to her sultry voice and grow drowsy with the two infants before she put me to bed and used her mouth in other ways.

"Yes, we want the story of you and Mummy!" Kes looked at his sister. "True story, right, Em?"

Emma clapped her hands. "True. True!"

Vaughn muttered under his breath. "God, I think you're a small statistic of parents who should never tell their kids how they met. It's not like you shacked up at some bar and made a drunken mistake—that's a bad enough tale to have, but mentioning a beheading for a debt from the 1400's...kind of far-fetched."

I chuckled. "It is far-fetched...but perhaps that's what makes it a good story?"

Jaz narrowed her eyes. "How do you mean?"

"I mean life isn't meant to be generic and follow a pre-approved script."

Nila murmured, "If it did, where would the adventures be...the dragon-slaying knights and unicorn-riding princesses?"

"I'm a princess," Emma announced, poking herself in the chest. "I am. Me."

I grinned indulgently. "And what sort of princess are you?"

She suddenly shot to her tiny feet and soared around the beanbags in her pink tutu with her arms stretched wide. "I'm a Hawk princess."

Nila grabbed her mid-run, tickling her and blowing raspberries on her neck. "A hawk, huh? Not an eagle or a kite or a vulture?"

Emma wrinkled her nose. "No, silly. A hawk." Pointing at me, Nila, and Kes, she said, "We're all Hawks."

Nila's thoughts tangled between marrying me and taking my last name and the fact that Jasmine would soon become a Weaver. We'd swapped roles. Blended our bloodlines.

Gathering my family closer, I said, "Okay, you want a story? I've got a story."

Instantly, the children hunkered down, their amber eyes locked on me. Jaz, V, and Nila placed me in the centre of attention, waiting for me to spin something crazy and fantastical.

But I wouldn't do that.

I wouldn't dishonour my children by lying to them, and I wouldn't discredit the past and not learn from history. They wanted to know the story of how Nila and I met? Okay, they'd hear the truth, and it was up to them to deem fact from fiction.

My children would be the opposite of what I'd been groomed to be. They would be kind and helpful; they'd never want for anything, but they would know how to help others less fortunate. They would be *better.*

"Once upon a time, there was a seamstress named Needle and Thread."

Emma sighed, snuggling closer to Nila. "She's like you, Mummy."

Kes shook his head defiantly. "She *is* Mummy."

My heart fisted with love. "That's right. Now, stop interrupting." Taking a deep breath, I hugged them harder. "One night, Needle had the largest party of her life. Kings and queens came from everywhere to see her magical creations with lace and cotton. She'd worked for years to create something so perfect and a dress that defied all beauty. A dress with feathers and diamantes and silk."

"And the naughty prince ripped it off her." Nila kissed my cheek, granting the secret words directly into my ear. "He threw her on his gallant steed and stole her into darkness."

Placing her head on my shoulder, she breathed, "But he

was already in love with her, so he'd lost the fight before it'd begun."

Kes and Emma couldn't hear what my incredible wife whispered, and I fought the urge to steal her away again and show her just how much I wanted her for eternity.

I fought the urge while my children waited for me to continue. But I couldn't tear my eyes away from Nila. "I was, you know."

She tensed, her eyes meeting mine. "You were? The text messages? They were enough to fall—"

"Fall in love with you? I think I fell in love with you when we met the final time when you were thirteen."

"I don't remember that."

"You wouldn't. I was supposed to say hello, but I couldn't ruin your day. You looked so happy. So I watched you in the park and gave my heart to you without even knowing it."

"Story! You're forgetting the story." Emma tugged on my sleeve, her face open and eager. "Please…"

Nila shifted in my arms, kissing me gently. "I loved you when you were Kite007. I loved you when you were Jethro Hawk, and I loved you when you finally became mine."

"Ewww." Kes stuck his tongue out.

With my soul about to split open with joy, I forced myself to ignore my wife and continue with the tale. Once the children were in bed and Jaz and V had gone, I'd spend the rest of the night showing Nila just how much I adored her and how glad I was that our story existed.

My voice threaded around the room, plaiting with the crackle of the fireplace. "Where was I? Oh yes, that's right. The dress Needle and Thread created was the most incredible thing anyone had ever seen. People offered to buy her castles and paradise for the chance to have her sew for them.

"Everything seemed right in the world, but Needle didn't know that a monstrous prince was coming for her. That he'd lied to her for months, sent secretive messages, and stolen her heart without her knowing." I paused for dramatics, squeezing

Kes and Emma tight. "He'd been sent to *hurt* her."

"No!" Emma squeaked.

"Oh, yes." I nodded sadly. "His task was to hunt her, hurt her, devour her."

Kes balled his tiny fists. "But you didn't let the bad prince take Mummy, did you?"

I lowered my voice, turning grave. "I did."

"No! Why?"

"Because...*I* was the bad prince. I'd been given a task to prove I was royal enough to inherit the realm and faraway castles, but no matter how bad I was, Needle had a magic I couldn't fight."

I settled into the soft bean-bag, diving committedly into the tale.

I wouldn't sugar-coat.

I'd tell them of the debts and pain. I'd gloss over things too old for their young ears, but I would ensure the message behind the history remained.

I believed everyone had a tolerance for darkness because life wasn't just light. Life wasn't rainbows and bunny rabbits nor good luck or easy fortune. Real life was hard. There was mess and lies and heartbreak. They deserved to know they'd suffer tragedies as well as triumphs. They needed to be equipped to deal with losing as well as winning. Because that was what made an empathic human over a monster.

And no matter how twisted and terrible our story had begun, our belief in love and tenderness turned fate's plan. Our dreams came true and were even more precious because of what we'd survived in order to earn it.

"There's darkness inside all of us." I glanced at my children, making sure they paid attention. "Some of us let it rule us. Some of us let it destroy us. And some of us rise to the challenge and fight it.

"All it takes is for that one person to believe that they're worthy. That we won't bow to poverty or hate or greed. That our life can be better than the shadows we let creep over it."

Emma nodded, but Kes turned sombre, turning over my words, soaking in the wisdom beneath.

Nila had won because she fought against the darkness.

And I'd won because I'd embraced my truth.

All it takes is for one of us to be brave enough to turn on the light.

"So the bad prince hurt Needle?" Emma whispered.

"Yes, he gave her to the trolls in the forest to extract tolls and payments for things she hadn't done."

"If she hadn't done them, then why could they do that?"

"Because they thought they were better than her and she owed them."

"That's mean." Emma pushed out her bottom lip. "Stupid trolls."

"I know," I agreed. "Very unfair and against every law of the land they lived in."

"So...what happened?" Kes asked, his face alight with interest.

"Yes, Kite, then what happened?" Nila brushed her lips across mine, her soul sewn completely to mine. "If the story started so cruelly, how does it end?"

I had the perfect answer.

The *only* answer.

The most brilliant thirteen-word reply ever uttered.

Kissing my wife and hugging my children, I murmured, "The only way such a tale can end...

...

They lived happily ever after."

Indebted Beginnings

COMING SOON

William Hawk's Tale & the Origins of the
Everything...

"It all began with greed and gluttony and ended with diamonds and guillotines. Debts were incurred, contracts were written, and a curse landed on the firstborns from both houses."

William Hawk was born into a family with vengeance rather than blood flowing in his veins. Against all odds, he transformed himself from pauper to Lord of Hawksridge. He became a smuggler, king's ally, and ruthless businessman. But he had flaws as well as triumphs.

It was those flaws that ruined his inheritance. Those flaws that saved him from himself. Those flaws that brought him the greatest wealth of all.
Her.

Do you want more Hawks? Do you want to know the deeper questions to the Debt Inheritance? Well, you've read Jethro and Nila's tale, now go back to the very beginning and read William's in INDEBTED BEGINNINGS.

About the Author

Pepper Winters is a New York Times and USA Today International Bestseller. She loves dark romance, star-crossed lovers, and the forbidden taboo. She strives to write a story that makes the reader crave what they shouldn't, and delivers tales with complex plots and unforgettable characters.

After chasing her dreams to become a full-time writer, Pepper has earned recognition with awards for best Dark Romance, best BDSM Series, and best Dark Hero. She's an #1 iBooks bestseller, along with #1 in Erotic Romance, Romantic Suspense, Contemporary, and Erotica Thriller. She's also honoured to wear the IndieReader Badge for being a Top 10 Indie Bestseller, and recently signed a two book deal with Hachette. Represented by Trident Media, her books have garnered foreign and audio interest and are currently being translated into numerous languages. They will be in available in bookstores worldwide.

Her Dark Romance books include:
Tears of Tess (Monsters in the Dark #1)
Quintessentially Q (Monsters in the Dark #2)
Twisted Together (Monsters in the Dark #3)
Debt Inheritance (Indebted #1)

First Debt (Indebted Series #2)
Second Debt (Indebted Series #3)
Third Debt (Indebted Series #4)
Fourth Debt (Indebted Series #5)
Final Debt (Indebted Series #6)
Indebted Epilogue (Indebted Series #7)

Her Grey Romance books include:
Destroyed
Ruin & Rule (Pure Corruption #1)

Upcoming releases are:
Sin & Suffer (Pure Corruption #2)
Je Suis a Toi (Monsters in the Dark Novella)
Unseen Messages (Contemporary Romance)
Super Secret Series
Indebted Beginnings

To be the first to know of upcoming releases, please follow her on her website
Pepper Winters

She loves mail of any kind: **pepperwinters@gmail.com**
All other titles and updates can be found on her
Goodreads Page.

Acknowledgements

(Deleted Sex Scene from Final Debt is after this section. Xx)

There are a few things I'd like to say now this series is complete. One, thank you for reading with me. For following Jethro and Nila through six books (really seven with the Epilogue) and (hopefully) enjoying their tale. As you've noticed, there is a lot of backstory and a rich world beyond their lives. I deliberately concentrated on Jethro and Nila's side of the story, so as not to get too confusing.

However, the longer I wrote *Indebted,* the more the past wanted to be told.

After writing Mabel and William's side when Cut is in the mine with Nila, it's made me want to revisit the beginning and truly dive deeper into the trials and hardships endured by both sides.

Indebted Beginnings will follow William as he builds Hawksridge, sets up an empire, and falls into his own pitfalls of life. I don't have a release date yet but can't wait to write his tale and answer any other questions you have about the series.

Now that's out of the way, let's talk about other things.

The stabbing with Daniel and the knitting needle.
Believe it or not, that is based on a true fact. In my family

line—I won't say if it's my lineage or my husband's side—a wife killed her husband using a knitting needle. She was tried and convicted of manslaughter after a long case of confusion. The puncture to his heart was barely noticeable and most doctors back then thought it was a heart attack. (Just in case you thought that wasn't possible, it's based on fact.)

There are also a few other things in the story that are real. I, myself, suffer from vertigo. Not nearly as bad as Nila, but I know first-hand what her symptoms are like.

Now, onto the acknowledgments.

Thank you so much to Amy K Jones for being so likeminded as me. Yaya for being so honest. Tamicka for laying her thoughts out so concisely. Melissa for printing off Final Debt and reading in paper form. Vickie for keeping me going with awesome messages. Skye for being my daily writing partner for over two years. The ladies in FUNK who are the most inspiring bunch of women I know. Lisa for arranging my blog tours and handling PR. Kellie for the epic boxed set covers for Indebted. Ari for the awesome single covers for Indebted. Celesha for making some incredible teasers for this series. Jenny for her quick editing skills. Ellen for her fast proofreading. Erica for her eagle-eye proofreading. Selena for running my groups and my life so well. Katrina for her wealth of industry titbits and knowledge. My husband for sticking with me and encouraging me to write even when the beginning was rocky. And to every reader who gave this saga a try and enjoyed—to every reader who gave it a try and didn't. To every blogger, reviewer, friend, and confidant. Your messages and help and kindness truly make my life so much more rounded and happy.

I know I've forgotten people but my brain always goes on the fritz when doing these acknowledgements, hence why I don't do them often anymore as I'm terrified of leaving people out.

Lastly, I thought I'd answer a few questions that had been

asked over the past year while writing the Indebted Series. Now that it's finished, I can shed light on any last minute questions and spend a little longer in the Indebted world.

Do you love knowing that you reach your fans on such a deep level when they read your books?

Yes, I'm beyond awed that I'm able to create an emotional response through words. I'm constantly grateful for messages saying they truly felt a scene or character. Nothing means more to me than that.

Will we get spinoff stories/prequel to this AMAZING series?

Yes, *Indebted Beginnings* will be released soon (no date as yet) and I might do a few more if the story strikes me. The history is very rich and a lot of avenues to explore.

Who did you vision as Nila and Jethro?

I don't have an actor or actress in mind at the moment. But if you have someone in mind, email me and show me.

Who was your favourite character to bring alive? Who did you hate most?

My favourite was definitely Jethro as he had such a multifaceted character to bring out. Hate? Hard to tell because even if the characters were evil in the book, their strong opinions made it easy to write. I guess…Daniel was the hardest as I actually felt sorry for him and how he was treated.

Will there be audio books coming?

Yes, these are being created as we speak and will be out in early 2016, you can listen to a snippet **HERE**

Will you do signed paperbacks of this series?

Yes, you can order them from my website **HERE**. I'll also have limited edition boxed sets. Debt Inheritance, First Debt,

Second Debt in one edition, and Third Debt, Fourth Debt, Final Debt, Indebted Epilogue in another as there are too many pages for one complete book.

Who was the toughest character to write about? Who was the easiest?

I sort of answered this above but Jethro was easiest because I always knew who he was. Maybe the hardest was Kestrel because I fell in love with him and always knew his fate so it was bittersweet.

Can you please create a lineage of all Hawks and Weavers back to when the Hawks were given the document by the Queen. Would like to see the whole family tree - even if there are mysteries.

Yes, I'll work on something like this to insert in *Indebted Beginnings*. I won't share yet as if I do spinoffs I don't want too many spoilers revealed too early.

This story is EPIC! Why is HBO or Starz not working on the TV show already!!? Seriously!

I would LOVE to see this as a TV Series. If I can make it happen, I will.

What do you have coming next, can you share with us?

I have a LOT coming in 2016. *Sin & Suffer* will be released on the 26th January 2016 and will complete the Pure Corruption Series. It will be in book stores and online. *Unseen Messages* will be my next release which I'm DYING to show you the cover and blurb. On the 20th December, I'll reveal the insanely beautiful cover on my website. In January, I'll also release the blurb and cover for the Super Secret Series I'll be publishing in 2016. I'm BEYOND excited to share and have already fallen in love with these characters. Je Suis a Toi will be coming in 2016, too.

Will you be at any signings in 2016?
Not at this stage. I'm going to be focusing on writing as much as possible and building a home with my husband. I hope to travel again in 2017.

You mentioned a deleted sex scene from Final Debt, where is that?
Keep scrolling. It's a few pages away from here.

If you have any other questions please email **pepperwinters@gmail.com** or join the **Indebted Group Read** on Facebook to share with other readers.

I haven't forgotten that I promised sneak peeks into **Unseen Messages** and **Sin & Suffer**…here is a little taster:

Unseen Messages

(Please sign up for release day alerts and my website to be the first to see the cover and learn of a publishing date)

LIFE OFFERS EVERYONE messages.

Either unnoticeable or obvious, it's up to us to pay attention.

I didn't pay attention.

Instinct tried to take notice; the world tried to prevent my downfall.

I didn't listen.

I will forever wonder what would've happened if I did pay attention to those messages. Would I have survived? Would I have fallen in love? Would I have been happy?

Then again, perhaps just like messages existed, fate existed, too.

And no matter what life path we chose, fate always had the final say.

I didn't listen but it doesn't mean I didn't live.

I just lived a different tale than the one I'd envisioned.

Away from my home.

Away from my family.

But I wasn't alone…

I was with him.

And he became my entire universe.

Sin & Suffer

HE WAS A BULLY.
Ever since his voice deepened he'd mean and short-tempered. Mom told me that he was at a point in his life where he had to lose himself to find himself. I had no idea what she meant. I just...I just really missed my best-friend. —Diary entry, Cleo, age nine.

* * *

AMNESIA.

A curse or a blessing?

Memory.

A helping hand or hindrance?

The things I'd forgotten and remembered had been both enemy and friend—solace and pain. They'd been constant companions, fighting over me for years. Amnesia traded my first life for a new one—with new parents, new sister, new home. But then the boy with the green eyes brought me back—showed me the path to my old world and a destiny I'd forgotten.

For eight years I'd struggled, always fearing I'd left loved ones behind. I'd hated myself for being so selfish—knowing my brain had deliberately cut them out in an act of self-preservation. I'd always wondered what I would do when I finally remembered everything...*if* I finally remembered.

I didn't have to wonder anymore.

Even after the consequences of following a mysterious letter, the snake pit of lies, the confusion of blended pasts, the rough way Killian had treated me—I wouldn't change a thing.

Those trials were a worthy payment for my broken memories. I was whole again...*almost.*

As a final note, I'd like to say thank you again for reading. I'll never stop being awed that this is my career and forever humbled that people enjoy my work. I write for you and hope to deliver many more books for decades to come.

THANK YOU.

(Keep reading for the deleted sex scene from Final Debt)

Other Book Blurbs & Reviews

<u>26th January 2016</u>
Sin & Suffer (Pure Corruption MC #2)

"Some say the past is in the past. That vengeance will hurt both innocent and guilty. I never believed those lies. Once my lust for revenge is sated, I'll say goodbye to hatred. I'll find a new beginning."
Buy Now

<u>2016</u>
Je Suis a Toi (Monsters in the Dark Novella)

"Life taught me an eternal love will demand the worst sacrifices. A transcendent love will split your soul, cleaving you into pieces. A love this strong doesn't grant you sweetness—it grants you pain. And in that pain is the greatest pleasure of all."
Buy Now

<u>Early 2016</u>
Unseen Messages (Standalone Romance)

"I should've listened, should've paid attention. The messages were there. Warning me. Trying to save me. But I didn't see and I paid the price..."
Get Release Day Alerts when this Book is Published

Early 2016
Super Secret Series Starting Soon

Please keep an eye out for the blurb and cover reveal early 2016. I'm beyond excited about this series and hope to deliver another epic tale.

"He has millions, but without her he is bankrupt.
And he'll spend every dollar and penny to get her back."
Get Release Day Alerts when this Book is Published

Tears of Tess (Monsters in the Dark #1)

"My life was complete. Happy, content, everything neat and perfect.
Then it all changed.
I was sold."
Buy Now

Quintessentially Q (Monsters in the Dark #2)

"All my life, I battled with the knowledge I was twisted… screwed up to want something so deliciously dark—wrong on so many levels. But then slave fifty-eight entered my world. Hissing, fighting, with a core of iron, she showed me an existence where two wrongs do make a right."
Buy Now

Twisted Together (Monsters in the Dark #3)

"After battling through hell, I brought my esclave back from the brink of ruin. I sacrificed everything—my heart, my mind, my very desires to bring her back to life. And for a while, I thought it broke me, that I'd never be the same. But slowly the beast is growing bolder, and it's finally time to show Tess how beautiful the dark can be."
Buy Now

Destroyed (Standalone Grey Romance)

She has a secret.
He has a secret.
One secret destroys them.
Buy Now

Ruin & Rule (Pure Corruption MC #1)

"We met in a nightmare. The in-between world where time had no power over reason. We fell in love. We fell hard. But then we woke up. And it was over . . ."
Buy Now

Deleted Scene from Final Debt

Deleted Scene taken from Final Debt *after the bonfire of burning torture relics and Weaver files. Instead of leaving it forever on my hard drive, it's here for you to read if you wish.*

Hope you enjoy…

MY COCK SWELLED as her hands grazed my chest, disappearing to unbuckle my belt. I didn't pull away as she undid my jeans and reached into my boxer-briefs to fist around my rapidly hardening length.

I groaned as her thumb smeared over the crown, pressing with perfect pressure. "Nila…"

"I need you, Kite." Her lips never left mine. "I need you to remind me I'm alive after so many of those we love are dead."

I pulled back.

Her face tracked with tears, shattering my heart. This was supposed to be a happy time, and yet we'd all been sucked into sadness.

Looping my fingers in the strands of her smoke-laced hair, I whispered, "Anything. Tell me how to make you come alive and I'll do it." I kissed her. "I'll do anything you need."

Her face darkened with desire so furious, I sucked in a breath. "That night you taught me how it was for you. The intensity lesson and the way you made me focus on the simplest of things."

My lips twisted even as my heart leapt in lust. "My whip?"

She bit her lip, nodding. "I want that again. I want to remember we're still here. That our love is still real and no matter what, we won. I need reminding we have our entire lives to spend together. It doesn't matter how we came together; nothing can ever tear us apart."

I couldn't help myself. I kissed her excruciatingly hard. "You're a witch, I swear. Or maybe a HSP yourself. "

She frowned. "How do you mean?"

"I need the same thing." I smiled, tracing her bottom lip with my finger. "I feel like I've lost you a little. That you doubt what we have is true. I need to make you focus. To accept nothing else could match what we've found. And in a way, I need to punish you for ever doubting that."

I stared at her with a mixture of awe and worship. Had she picked up on my silent wishes as I picked up on hers? Last week, while dealing with Bonnie's funeral and lawyer documents, I'd had the sudden compulsion to fight such grief with blistering dirty sex. I wanted to ravage and fuck. I wanted to remind myself that no matter what I'd done to my father, I was still me and still deserving of Nila's love.

I hadn't asked her to give me what I needed as I hadn't wanted to hurt or upset her.

But here she was asking for the same thing.

"You're fucking perfect." I kissed her.

"And you." She kissed me back.

"Will you let me have control tonight? Let me do what we both need?"

Her head fell back, submitting to me. "Anything, Jethro. I'm yours for the night. Do anything you want."

"Just the night?"

A sly smile spread her lips. "You want more than that?"

The growl built in my throat. "You know I do."

"In that case, you better prove to me you can love me

enough to last forever."

More than forever, Needle.

I didn't hesitate.

Letting her go, I shot to my drawers and pulled out two ties. Both silver with diamonds spilling down the fabric.

Nila didn't take her eyes off me as I prowled to the head of the bed and snapped my fingers. The old hint of authority sent a shiver down her spine. "Come here, Ms. Weaver."

She obeyed faster than any order when I'd been deadly serious. My lips quirked.

Seems sex is more wanted than debts.

My heart tripped.

If she reacted so defiantly and strong when facing something she didn't want to face, what would she be like in our future? Would she be eager to do things I could guarantee she'd love? Could we finally have the trust I'd always begged her to give me so I could live entirely in her feelings for me?

Biting my lip, I ran the two ties through my fingers. "You're making it very hard to remember I should be punishing you and not rewarding you."

She smiled as she lay back, placing her hands above her head. Licking her lips, she never took her eyes from mine. "Perhaps, I want both."

I swallowed hard, climbing on the bed and hovering over her. Slinging my knee over her hips, I straddled her.

We didn't stop staring; my mouth watered, my cock hardened, and the shitty night faded. Somehow, she even managed to stop me thinking about Kestrel's funeral in a few hours, about the mammoth task before me of culling the mine and granting peace to a scarred nation, and all the loose ends I had to tie up now I was heir.

I'm heir.

I never thought I'd say the words.

Hawksridge is mine.

Once upon a time, that was all I wanted because it offered freedom for my siblings and me. But now…I could walk away from it tomorrow because Nila was my true freedom and I loved her more than any estate or bank balance.

Dropping over her, I kissed her quickly, forcing myself not to get carried away. Her hand swooped up to my cheek, caressing me with love and lust.

Pulling back, I dropped the ties to the mattress and tugged on the hem of her glittery blue jumper. "This needs to come off."

Sitting up in one sweep like a ballerina, she let me pull the fabric over her head. She didn't say a word as I removed the small tank top underneath and unhooked her bra.

Once I'd revealed her breasts, her nipples instantly hardened, begging me to bite and suck.

I deliberately brushed my knuckles over them, granting her a smidgen of pleasure.

She gasped, her black eyes turning into empty galaxies just waiting for me to give her an orgasm and fill them with stars.

My cock twitched, begging to take her. But I had something to do first.

Picking a single tie from beside my knee, I growled, "Put your hands together."

She stiffened with anticipation but obeyed. Her elegant fingers latched together, presenting them to me like the perfect surrender.

Taking her wrists, I gently wrapped the silver tie around her, securing it tight but not too tight. Guiding her arms back to rest on the pillow above her head, I kissed her brow. "Keep them there. Do not move. Understand?"

Her pulse echoed in her throat, dancing beneath her diamond collar. "I understand."

"Good girl."

Resting back on my knees, I turned my attention to her trousers. I tapped her hips. "These need to go, too." My voice no longer resembled a distinguished lord, more like a feral sex-starved man who desperately wanted to fuck.

"Of course." Nila arched her back, holding herself with

suburb muscles as I unbuttoned and unzipped her jeans. A soft pant fell from her lips as I wrenched the denim down her legs, followed by her lacy knickers.

Naked.

Was there anything more fucking perfect than Nila naked, willing, and wet in my bed?

Fuck.

She looked positively decadent.

My hands curled, forcing myself to find some restraint from fucking her that very instant. Tracing my finger along the inside of her thigh, I murmured, "Now, Ms. Weaver...what, oh what, should I do with you?"

Her skin flushed as her eyes dropped to my fully dressed body. "I want to see you."

I shook my head. "You have to deserve that. I think you need to do a few more things for me before that, don't you?"

Her midnight eyes darkened impossibly further. "Like what?"

"I can think of a few things."

Climbing down her body, I placed my elbows on the bed, settling myself between her spread legs. My chin hovered over her cunt, my eyes locked on hers. "I'm going to taste you, Nila. I'm going to make you explode and show you you're alive and with me and safe. Foreign sisters don't matter. Mother's secrets don't matter. All that matters is *us.*"

Nila panted as I bowed over her and breathed hot on her clit. My breath misted her delicate skin, heating her core, making her moan.

She bucked in my arms. "Oh, my God." Her bound hands flew to her chest, struggling against the knotted tie.

Grabbing her silk-covered wrists, I clucked my tongue. "Put those back above your head."

She gasped, struggling to obey when every nerve ending existed in her pussy.

Slowly, she rested her arms back on the pillow. Smirking, I lowered my mouth, licking her quick and sharp.

"Oh…" She shuddered.

I licked her again, absorbing her taste, struggling with my own resolve to grant her pleasure when all I wanted was to climb inside her. "More?"

Her head tossed back, another moan responding in answer.

My muscles stiffened. My cock ached in my jeans. I wanted to forget all pretence and just fuck this woman. Claim her as mine. But she wanted to come alive. I would do everything in my power to make that happen.

I'd make her cry with hysteria. I'd make her laugh at how good it felt to breathe and let me control her pleasure.

Slipping fingertips between her legs, I traced my way upward. Every sweep of my tongue and inch of my fingers, she trembled and tensed.

The higher I got, the more her legs forced to close, clamping around my shoulders.

Shaking my head, I speared the tip of my tongue into her folds. Grabbing her legs, I slammed them open, pressing them into the mattress, ensuring she was bared, exposed, and entirely vulnerable to whatever I wanted to do to her.

"Stay, Needle. Otherwise, my tongue will become teeth."

She groaned—it echoed through the bed, hypnotising me.

Her pussy glistened, so wet with need.

Dragging a finger though her slickness, I murmured, "You want me so much, Ms. Weaver."

"You know I do."

"Tell me."

Her voice was a husky whisper. "Tell you what?"

"Tell me how much you need me."

She gasped as I inserted the tip of my finger inside her. "So much. Too much. Way, *way* too much."

Her muscles leapt beneath my touch, both externally and internally.

In our bedroom, there was nothing else to think about. Here, it was just us. A place devoid of people. We were in our own world. A world filled with love and lust and a connection so strong, I could come just from her thoughts. From living her pleasure and what I did to her.

It was the strangest, most surreal sensation.

The intimacy of the moment swamped me with everlasting joy. Her feet rubbed on the sheets as my tongue landed on her exposed core. Her hands opened and closed in the binds, her hips rocking into my mouth.

My only goal was to please her and show how much I fucking adored her. Not just for tonight or tomorrow but every night and day in our future.

I sucked her clit, unsheathing my teeth to nibble. My hips pistoned, pressing my hard dick into the mattress, seeking relief as her taste exploded through my veins.

"I'm so grateful for you, Nila."

Her head thrashed as my voice resonated through my tongue and into her pussy. "I'll spend the rest of my life making sure you know how damn grateful I am."

My hips rocked harder, fucking the bed as desire built swift and demanding in my blood. Sliding over her, I licked her nipple, sucking the hardened flesh into my mouth.

She cried out, her skin flushing with sweat. "Jethro—"

"What do you want?"

"I want—I want—"

Then a thought popped into her head, and I caught it. I caught the explosion of desire, asking me to do something she daren't verbalize. Lucky for her, I sensed what she needed.

I obeyed.

Baring my teeth, I bit her nipple.

Hard.

She moaned loudly in reward, telling me without words that I understood exactly what she wanted. Tonight, she didn't want sweet or soft. Tonight, she wanted to be marked and ridden. To feel human and come alive with aches and love-bruises and the knowledge she'd wake up tomorrow with memories of what we did in the dark.

I would oblige her completely.

Starting from her lips, I kissed her hot and deep. My teeth captured her lip, biting down so she would feel my kiss long after I left to bestow attention on other parts.

Trailing from her mouth to her throat, I bit her.

From throat to collarbone, I bit and licked and loved.

Every inch of her body, I bit.

Leaving indents of my teeth for a few seconds before her flushed skin absorbed the erotic pain, begging for more.

"I love your tiny breasts, you know that?" I swirled my tongue around her nipple remembering the first time I saw her. The awful things I said to her. The barely delivered lies about needing a woman with bigger breasts and more confidence.

I'd been enthralled with her from the very first moment. I'd just done a better job of hiding my true desires back then.

She laughed, her skin quaking beneath my tongue. "I'll have to go back over what you've said to me and see how much was real and what was fake."

I chuckled, biting my way down her stomach, nipping each rib, ensuring every inch of her was tasted. "Most was a lie. When I told you I couldn't stand you, I really meant I loved you. When I said you drove me mad, I really meant I wanted you more than I could breathe."

Her eyes met mine, liquid with love. "Jethro…"

I smiled lopsidedly. "You had to have guessed how insanely hard I fell for you? Those first texts, the First Debt. Fuck, Nila. It took every willpower not to steal you away then and there."

Tearing my gaze away, I bit her particularly hard on her hipbone, dragging a strangled cry from her lips. "I'm going to punish you for that. Reprimand you for the power you've always held over me."

She moaned as my mouth latched over her pussy again, only this time, I didn't just lick; I fucked her with my tongue, lavishing her with my teeth.

Her fingers clenched in the tie, her back arching for more.

Planting a hand on her lower belly, I kept her in place as I licked and laved, forcing her to peak fast and hard.

"Oh, shit!"

Her legs locked. "I'm…I'm—"

Her belly fluttered. "Don't stop. Don't—"

"Fuuuck." Her pussy rippled around my tongue.

Her orgasm sparked from nothing, exploding with fireworks. My tongue drank up every clench, and I didn't stop until she fell limp against the bed.

My chin and lips smeared with her pleasure as I stared up her svelte body, smiling at her wanton happiness. "Are you feeling alive yet, Ms. Weaver?"

She wriggled, her skin flushing. "I'm starting to."

"Only starting to? I better increase my efforts."

Climbing up her body, I hovered over her. Impossibly, I fell even more in love with her. Tucking hair from her eyes, I undid the tie around her wrists. "Now, what do you suggest I do with you?"

Her black hair tangled on the pillow as she shrugged, rolling her wrists in their newfound freedom. "Anything your heart desires."

A grumble sounded low in my chest. "Giving me carte blanche is a dangerous thing."

"No, it's not."

"Why?"

"Because I trust you, Jethro. I trust you with my heart and soul."

Gritting my jaw, I looked away. She understood me so fucking much. Closing my eyes, I gathered my control. If I let myself give in, I'd be inside her within seconds before we had a chance to fully embrace the alchemy between us.

I groaned as Nila shifted onto her knees. "I know what else you can do." With fluttering hands, she undressed me like I'd undressed her. Her fingers kissed my lower belly, gathering the hem of my black t-shirt and ripping it over my head. "You can make love to me, so I can return the favour you just gave me."

Tossing the material onto the floor, her expert touch descended on my jeans. "I want to touch you, fuck you, and keep you forever." Her talent as a seamstress undid the fastening faster than I ever could, her hands hot on my hips as she shoved my jeans and boxer-briefs down in one go. "Move so I can get rid of these."

I didn't speak, lapping up everything she gave.

Rolling onto my back, I copied what she'd done and arched.

Her tongue came out, licking her bottom lip as her eyes locked on my hard dick, slipping my clothing off me and to the floor.

Naked.

Both of us this time.

Time stopped ticking onward. The new day paused. And Nila and I just stared.

Our promises of intensity and taking it slow hovered like scripture, slowly disintegrating the longer we breathed.

I wanted her so fucking much.

Her hand landed on my cock.

And that was it.

I couldn't do it anymore.

I didn't know who moved first.

One second, I was on my back, the next, my hands were full of Nila's hair and my mouth connected with hers.

We threw ourselves together.

Our bodies slammed into one.

Nothing else mattered but joining.

The whip and ties would have to wait for another time. This...this didn't need props or toys. This was pure undulated passion.

The sheets tangled around my legs as I imprisoned her on her back.

Her chest rose and fell, her breasts squashing deliciously against my chest. "God, Kite..."

Words.

Words weren't allowed when all I wanted was emotion.

She could talk to me but in silent form. She could beg me but only in her mind. I would hear. I would understand. And I would fucking deliver every command she decreed.

My lips captured hers again. My mind focused on nothing but the rhythmic strokes of her taste, her fingernails slicing down my spine for more.

Somehow, our legs entwined, our arms plaited, our entire bodies fought to get closer. Her legs spread wider, her knees nudging mine as she cradled me between them.

I wanted her like that.

I wanted her rough. Gentle. Safe. Dangerous.

But in that second, I needed her brutal.

She needed me to bite her?

Well, I needed to fuck her.

Shooting upward, I grabbed her hot skin, flipping her onto her front. "Tell me now if this is going to be a problem."

Sitting on her knees, she arched her spine, standing on all fours. The dip of her spine blew my fucking mind, the crack of her arse leading the way to the hottest wettest cunt I'd ever had.

Looking over her shoulder, her lips burned bright red, swollen from our kisses. Her face flushed pink from her orgasm and her thoughts...they gave me complete freedom to take her like this.

She wanted it.

"You want to be ridden?"

She bit her lip, her teeth indenting the red flesh. "More than anything."

Swallowing a possessive growl, I clamped one hand on her hips and the other around my cock. Yanking her backward, I positioned myself to line up perfectly.

As her entrance locked over the crown of my cock, I couldn't see. My eyes short-circuited as insane bliss catapulted down my dick and into my balls.

I had her in my arms, and yet, somehow, I still expected

her to vanish.

She was everything I ever dreamed of. I couldn't help fearing she'd be gone when I woke. I'd find she never existed and this was all a terrible fantasy.

But then she rocked backward, sliding her pussy down my length. Her spine rolled, her head folding toward the bed.

"More."

Shit, I'd give her more.

I'd give her everything.

Thrusting upward, her body offered no barrier as I filled her completely. Her previous orgasm slicked and prepared her. I didn't have to worry about being gentle or slow. I could climb inside and take everything she offered.

Leaning forward, I wrapped my arm around her chest. My hand grabbed her dangling breasts, squeezing the weight. My mouth found her spine, kissing the beads of her bones, thrusting again and again.

Opening myself to every thought of Nila's, I felt her gratitude, her love, her desire. I felt her happiness, her singular concentration on me inside her, and the quietness that being together brought.

Biting her waist, I continued to thrust upward. My hips rocking to a punishing rhythm, forcing Nila to match my pace, slamming us together, keeping our bodies joined.

"Fuck, you feel so good." I kissed and bit her, driving myself insane with sensation. "I want to come all over you. In you. On you. I want you like this for the rest of our lives. I want you to know you belong to me. I need you. Shit, I need you."

Her voice wobbled, breathless with our pace. "Don't stop."

My balls tightened, building with bubbling pressure. My cock grew thicker and harder, impaling her, spearing her, diving into her over and over and *over.*

My hands roamed over her back and waist. I couldn't stop touching her. Fisting her short hair, I rode her hard and fast.

Degrading but respecting. Cruel but loving.

"I stole you from everyone. I snapped the collar around your neck and made you mine. Every scream you uttered is mine. Every moan you've made is mine. Your heart beats for *mine*. Fuck, Nila."

Her neck curved backward as I kept tight hold of her hair. "Yes. God, yes."

My legs trembled, my knees glued to the mattress as I thrust again and again.

My release gathered in every cell, electrifying together, surging into my cock.

Sweat misted my hairline as I continued to ravage. My fingers bruised her hips as I yanked her back again and again. "I'll never stop needing you, Needle. I want to know your every secret. I want to grow old with you. I want to be the reason you smile and hurt those who make you cry. I want you by my side when I finally do something worthwhile, and I want to enjoy every fucking second we have left together."

Nila's flesh bounced, her thighs cracking with mine as I hurtled toward the finish. Reaching between her legs, I strummed her clit, forcing her to climb to the heights of where I was.

I wanted to come. Fuck, how I wanted to come.

But I wanted her there with me.

A short cry fell from her lips as her back stiffened. Her fingernails dug into the mattress, forcing me to fuck her harder, touch her faster.

"Yes, yes…yes."

The pleasure was too great.

The pressure too demanding.

I couldn't wait.

Plastering my sweaty skin on hers, I hollowed my cheeks, sucking her skin, kissing her, biting her. My fingers worked her clit as my hips spasmed in a brutal finish.

Shards of pain erupted up my legs morphing into the sharpest bliss I'd ever had as the first spurt splashed into her.

"God, Nila."

I reared up, throwing my head back as another wave erupted. And another. And another. Goosebumps decorated my skin as every rapture transferred from me to my woman.

Nila came.

Her screams merged with my grunts. Her pussy milking me as my orgasm crested.

We continued rocking long after the adrenaline and intensity of shared releases faded. We didn't speak as I let go of her hair, massaging her shoulders, running my fingers over her spine.

Together, we flopped to the side, letting the mattress cradle us.

I didn't withdraw and the combined heat and wetness inside her bound us even more.

Spooning Nila, I grabbed the covers and tugged it over us. Her skin chilled quickly after the heat of sex. Nuzzling her from behind, I cupped her breast and sucked in a huge gust.

"Come closer." My voice was hoarse; my touch gentle after being merciless.

She snuggled backward, her head on my arm as I became her pillow. "Any closer and I'll be inside you."

I sighed. "You already are."

"Tell me again."

My eyes closed, sated and emotionally drained. "Tell you what?"

She waited, feathering out her thoughts for me to catch. In a strange way, I would be her very own dream catcher, sorting through her wishes while she slumbered, doing my best to make them true while she was awake.

My body quivered with residual spasms. The aftershocks of pleasure were almost as enjoyable as the finale. "You're so stunning." I kissed her shoulder.

"Not that." She squirmed, laughing softly.

"You're so dirty in bed."

"Not that, either." Her head turned; the slice of tiny teeth marked my wrist.

"Ow." I squeezed her, chuckling. "Kiss me and I'll tell you what you want to hear."

Slowly, she turned her head. Her hips arched, curving into me. My cock remained hard inside her, wanting to take her all over again.

Her lips sealed over mine, her tongue slipping soundlessly into my mouth. The joining was erotic, sated, promised, free. I held her there. Kissing her, breathing her, communicating without messy sounds.

For now and every moment in our future, we were inseparable.

My teeth sank into her swollen bottom lip, granting what she wanted. "I love you."

Her eyes opened, black and glowing. "How much?"

"As much as the universe but not as much as infinity."

Her forehead furrowed. "What does that mean?"

"It means infinity states a reference of time, regardless if it means never ending. I like to think there is no linear equation or quantifiable way to love you. So I love you as much as love itself which really has no assessment."

She smiled. "You're so strange."

"You've only just noticed?"

She laughed. Her pussy clutched my cock, sending a wave of need into my balls. "Oh, I've noticed. I also noticed you're completely insane, mad—bonkers even. What did I call you? A loony toon?"

"I think you called me a Nutcase Hawk."

"That fits, too."

"I did warn you not to call me crazy."

"Turns out, I'm the one who's crazy."

My lips curled, knowing where she was going but happy to oblige the punch line. "Oh?"

Her hand drifted to mine, looping our fingers together, sighing happily. "Crazy in love with you." Kissing my knuckles, she settled into the bed and my arms. "We can be mad together, Kite. Because together it's the best form of insanity there is."

Thank you so much for reading.

Made in United States
Troutdale, OR
11/19/2024

25078182R00083